Comments & Reviews from Previous Books:

"Just finished *High Country Adventure*. I enjoyed it VERY much. A good book and a very good writer!" 89 year old Missouri man.

"When will the sequel be out?" female reader.

"I finished it in two days of reading," eleven year old girl.

"Each one gets better than the one before," female reader.

"It is the kind of book I could read again and again," female reader.

"I like the way you slip history into the story," male reader.

"Just got through reading your book *Child of the Heart*. Was very good. As any good book, could not lay it down till done. Hope to read the rest of them soon.   Bev H."

"I am awaiting your next one as I really do enjoy reading them. Betty and Bill H." California

Who's the Boss?

Anita L. Allee

HISTORICAL NOVEL
SET IN BACA COUNTY, COLORADO

1886-1889

ISBN: 1-59196-754-6

Published in the US by Instant Publisher.com

PO Box 985, Colliersville, TN 38027

This is a work of fiction based upon historic fact with similar incidents from my grandmother's childhood.

Ultimate design, content and editorial accuracy of this work is the responsibility of the author. Scripture references are paraphrased by the characters from the King James Version of the Bible.

Publisher's cataloging-in-publication

    Allee, Anita L.

        1. Early History in Baca County, Colorado.

        2. Homesteading/ranching

    Fiction-title

Printed in the United States of America by

InstantPublisher.com

Contact at: anviallee@earthlink.com

Dedication:

Anita's paternal grandmother, Pearl C. Butler Gatson, assisted her family in homesteading for ten years in southeastern Colorado near the western Kansas border. They farmed more than ranched on their homestead.

Their 320 acre homestead, improvements, and livestock, sold for $600.00 when they gave up. That was much less than their original cost.

The Butler family Colorado homestead bordered one branch of the Santa Fe Trail and was in sight of Two Buttes, built from the tailings left from an earlier mining operation. The family traded at the boom town of Minneapolis, Grandmother Pearl attended Minneapolis school, and one of her half brothers clerked in a store there.

Grandmother Pearl at eighteen years of age, drove a covered wagon east, *back* to Missouri, when her family returned after several years of drought drove them from their homestead along with thousands of other displaced farmers who were ill-prepared for dryland farming.

After the family's homesteading adventures, the Butlers built a house in Missouri, nearly identical to the one they had built and left in Baca County, Colorado.

In Ralls County, Missouri, Anita's grandmother Pearl and grandfather, James Thomas Gatson, established the farm on which Anita and her siblings were born. They were reared nearby where her grandmother's Butler family lived out their lives. Anita's father, Willoughby Henry Gatson, farmed this land and attended the one room Butler School, as did all four of his children. One of Pearl's great grandsons now owns the Butler farm.

Anita grew up listening to her grandmother's tales of her family homesteading during her years from eight to eighteen.

This book is in tribute to the Butler and Gatson families' tenacity and hard work. I am indebted to them for their continued faith in God and strong American heritage.

Who's the Boss? Characters

Jed Snowden - Ranch owner and boss

T.J. Smith - young financier

Aunt Mary Benton - T.J.'s widowed paternal aunt

"Shaker"-Ranch cook, hand, and horse doctor (Adam Shumate)

Max and Casey - ranch hands

Cleveland Oliver - Hometown Banker

Who's the Boss?

<u>Winter 1886-87 on the Open Plains of Southeast Colorado</u>

The relentless wind shrieked in Jed's head.

Lord, I can't hold on much longer.

He and his horse stood with their backs toward the stinging snow that bit to the very marrow of their bones. They were the perfect picture of misery, if they could have been seen through the chilling southwestern blizzard winds and the blowing snow that came straight from Canada and swept down through the Great Plains.

They were in the midst of a white-out. No living creature could see more than inches in front of its face.

The suffering animal's head drooped low. The big man touched her with a spur to keep moving.

"We'll freeze right here if we don't find a windbreak soon. Move," he mumbled through his frozen wool scarf. His eye lashes and brows were frosted, his eyes sticky. He could barely open them to squint against the driving snow that swirled around the pair.

He pulled the wool scarf higher over his face and ears. One loop wound over his hat. *Thank you mother for knitting this- you saved my face from freezing.*

The horse plodded on, sinking deeper and deeper into the gathering snow. The animal staggered, her legs slashed by the crust below the new and softer surface. She trudged on gamely. Blood stained her trail for only a moment before the wind blew the stains away or covered the traces.

Tired, we're so tired, can't go on.

Intermittently he roused to consciousness.

The snow blows through my clothes. I feel the icy splinters cut my skin.

The pair drifted ahead of the wind, the big rancher unsure of their destination or direction, their backs to the wind.

Can't see anything- can't find my way.

I'm too cold, don't care any more. Lord-   I'm in your hands, Jed whispered his last thought. He spiraled into oblivion as his horse drifted before the great blizzard of 1886. The one all the Great Plains would call the "Great Die-Up."

Hour after hour, the game but weakened animal plodded on before the howling blasts. Her rump tucked making herself as small toward the wind as possible, her tail tumbled around her hind legs. Long past the energy from her morning feed, her body drew heavily on her inner reserves. At times, she slipped and nearly went down.

Somehow the semi-conscious man stayed aboard, his natural instinct for survival and superb horsemanship victorious over the elements.

Finally the mare halted, unable to move further.

Jed roused to consciousness. His mind reacted sluggishly. He heard noises in the distance.

Where am I?

He thrashed out with his hands. *Surrounded by dark and warm, it seems warm. At least the wind's died down. It must be night. I left at dawn, must have been out here trying to shove the cattle to the hay ricks about twelve hours. Can't move my legs-   froze to the saddle.*

His horse shifted under him. Jed lifted his numbed arm to brush something from before his blinded eyes.

She's in the cedar windbreak next to the old soddy. Gotta move, try to get inside out of this cold. It's quiet now, but the temperature's dropping, we'll be froze before morning.

Jed clucked to his horse. The mare reluctantly stepped from their shelter. He guided the tough little buckskin toward the shed.

Can't get off. My legs won't work. With heavy arms, he shifted the reins to his right, toward the door of the cook shack. In the clear night sky, he could make out a thin stream of smoke rising from the chimney where his cook had banked the fire for the night.

He thumped the door. *Shaker has to be inside asleep by the big iron stove.*

The door opened a crack. A wild man in baggy long Johns peered out.

"Who's there?"

"It's me Shaker, can't get off my horse," Jed's voice was muffled by his frozen scarf.

"Boss?"

"Yeah."

"We thought you was a goner. Couldn't see nothin', didn't know where to go, no tracks out there-   we didn't go back out," Shaker apologized.

Jed groaned. "Can you help me?"

"Shur 'nough." The thin man reached for Jed. When his boss couldn't move, the cook pulled him from the horse. Both men sagged. Jed outweighed his friend by fifty pounds.

"Drag me inside and shut the door, maybe I can crawl over to the stove," Jed directed.

Shaker grabbed his boss under the arms and wrestled the bundle of heavy clothing inside the door. "Gotta get this door shut," he puffed with the exertion.

"Can't get my legs to work," Jed shifted using his arms. "Let me roll and I'll see if I can move myself. Don't want you to have a heart attack trying to move me."

The two panted, "I'm getting a few yards closer."

Shaker reached for his bed, "I'll get my blanket and drag you." He removed the heavy old buffalo robe from atop his thrown back bedding and placed it near his boss. Between himself and his boss' efforts, they piled the younger man onto the robe.

Shaker heaved. The robe edged along the rough floor boards. "We're makin' it."

"Thanks. Just toss another blanket over me and see if you can stir up a little heat," Jed said.

Shaker went to work tossing on shaved kindling and dry wood to make a quick, hot fire.

"There, think we got her goin'. I better see if I can get some of the hands and bring some more blankets. We'll take care of your horse."

Shaker continued, "You be all right while I'm gone?"

"Yeah, you do that." Jed closed his eyes and sank in relief.

Totally exhausted by his ordeal, he didn't hear the door open when Shaker had his coat on and went out into the still cold air of the night. He didn't see the glitter on the many new feet of drifted snow against the door.

The next sensation he felt was his legs burning unbearably. He thrashed, "My legs are on fire, must'a got too close to the stove."

"You all right, Boss?"

"My legs! They're on fire!" Jed groaned.

"You're thawin' out. It ain't gonna feel too good for a few hours, but I think the freezin' ain't too deep. Looks like your toes and fingers are fine."

Shaker looked at Jed's face, "You're gonna lose a little skin on your face, but that won't hurt you. Ain't no purty women out here to look at you no way."

Max and Casey looked subdued.

"I'm glad you can joke, it isn't funny," Jed groaned.

"We ain't jokin' just tryin' to keep your mind off it."

Jed struggled, "I gotta get up, can't stand my legs burning like this." He attempted to rise, sank back.

"Here, Boss, take my hand."

Shaker reached for one hand and Max the other arm.

"Can't seem to make my legs work," Jed groaned.

Shaker warned, "When you get on yur feet, they're gonna tingle and sting, but movin's gonna be good for you."

"Come on, Casey, Max, get under his shoulders. Let's heave him up and see if we can get him movin'."

The two staggered under their boss' weight, but began to move around in tiny circles inside the small cook shack.

Despite the cold outside, rivulets of perspiration dripped off Jed's chin and stung his eyes. He reached up and knuckled the sting from his eyes.

Shaker directed the two cowhands. He pointed his finger toward his bed, "Sit him there. I'll get a pan of water from the boiler and we'll warm him up."

The cook dipped water from the boiler he kept on the back of the stove. He tested with his forefinger, then turned and cracked ice on the water bucket. He reached for the long-handled dipper and poured a few cups of icy water into the big kettle, then tested the water again with his finger. *Just right.*

He threw the linen towel over his shoulder and knelt at his boss' feet.

"Here boys, peel up them pants and let's see what I can do." Shaker lifted a leg at the knee and placed the foot into the big kettle.

Excruciating pain racked through Jed's foot.

"Umh," he gritted his teeth to keep the cry inside. "Wait a minute, let me adjust."

Again perspiration broke out on his face. He knuckled it off his upper lip.

"Gotta go on boss, it'll make it better in the long run." Shaker dribbled water over the ankle and rinsed higher up the leg.

Jed gritted his teeth. The muscles in his neck stood out. He turned his head away from the men.

Uncomfortable, the hands shuffled their feet.

"I put your horse away, Boss. Covered her with a blanket."

"I thought you would. Sorry I couldn't do it for the ole girl. She brought me home. I got a lot to be grateful for, her included," Jed spoke through his gritted teeth.

"Sure was bad out there. Couldn't see no more, my horse got me back in 'bout noon," Max apologized.

"Glad you got in that soon, couldn't do any good out there after about ten this morning. Did the rest of the boys come in?" Jed asked.

"Yeah, we only got two other boys around. They all made it in. They're all fine," Casey said.

"Got all the cattle we could find in close as we could to the hay ricks. It's cleared off now, we should be able to take care of things, come mornin'."

His men seemed uncertain in this dire situation.

"Well, you boys better get some sleep. Shaker, you 'bout done there? I'm clear tuckered out. Maybe I can sleep a little too."

"Boss, take my bed, I'll roll up in this buffalo robe here by the fire."

"Don't want to take your bed," Jed said.

"Naw, I'm warmer here anyway. Sides, we don't want to get you too hot, you need to thaw out gradual or you'll suffer more in the long run."

"All right." Jed shifted his legs, then used his hands to help himself onto the wood frame.

The straw ticking rustled.

"Thanks boys. Shaker, you get some sleep now. We'll worry about the stock in the morning."

❊

Shaker rolled over as the boss shifted during the night.

"Need anythin', Boss?"

"Sorry, didn't aim to wake you."

"That's all right. Your legs botherin' you?

"Some."

"I know they must be. I got chilblains once, it ain't easy for a day or two. Hope it ain't too deep, or you're gonna have some open sores in a few days when the damage starts to slough off."

"It's nearly morning, get some sleep." Jed sounded gruff. *Don't want Shaker to know how bad I feel. He can't do anything else for me, gotta tough it out. Lord, can you help me with this? I'm not used to asking for myself, but this is rough.*

By morning Jed shifted restlessly, wracked with a climbing fever. He rolled back and forth, then threw the blankets off his arms and chest.

Shaker rose and bathed his boss' face and hands, then rolled back the edge of the blanket to check his feet. He pinched the skin lightly between his thumb and forefinger.

"I think we're gonna make it all right, may take a few days, but don't look like you're gonna lose much."

"I hope not, don't want to be a cripple depending on others," Jed said.

"That ain't likely," Shaker nodded.

❊

A month later, the crew still found dead stock on the range. Every slough, draw, and barrier held the dead animals, stacked atop each other where they'd stopped and others crowded in on them. Prairie varmints feasted on the thawing, then putrid carcasses.

"Well boys, that's all we can do. We got all the live ones situated around the ranch house and the food supply. I'm not coming back out on the range until the grass covers this mess," Jed directed the cowboys.

"Are you doin' all right, Boss?" Shaker asked.

"It'll have to do is about all I can say."

Financially strapped, but recovering physically, Jed went to the bank and asked for bank president, Cleveland Oliver.

After their conference, Mr. Oliver cleared his throat, "I can't grant more loans. I've already lent out all available money. I can't risk any more of the bank's money. What if we have a drought this summer, or another bad winter coming up?"

Jed twisted his hat, "That's in God's hands, but I'll do the best I can."

"I know you would. You have a reputation for being an honest, hard worker, but that doesn't change my situation here at the bank. I have responsibilities to many people. The board of directors have said, 'No more loans this spring.' I've even lent out all my own money I can spare. I want to save this town, but we could all go broke if this keeps up." Mr. Oliver rubbed his chin.

Jed turned to go.

The banker spoke, "Mr. Snowden, if you'd be interested in a private loan, I do have a client from further west. I've been acquainted with the family for sometime, they're honest folk. They came into town and have a little to invest."

"I'd consider any honest kind. Where do I go and who

do I see?" Jed asked.

"Go down to Mrs. Brown's rooming house and ask for T.J. Smith," Oliver replied.

"Thanks." Jed replaced his hat and turned for the door. "You won't regret telling me about where I can get a loan. I won't let your faith in me down, no matter what."

"If you'd like, I'll give you a personal recommendation to T.J." Oliver offered.

"I'd be grateful."

"I'll write it up and have it delivered."

Jed fidgeted while Mr. Oliver stepped through the side door of his office. The banker was gone several minutes.

Jed jumped to his feet when the door opened.

"I'll send it on it's way."

Mr. Oliver handed an envelope to a clerk.

"You can make the appointment at your convenience."

"Thank you, Sir."

Mr. Oliver reached for Jed's hand. "Good luck. Hope things go better for you in the future." The two men shook hands.

"I appreciate all this, thank you again," Jed placed his hat on his head and turned for the door.

Jed rode to Mrs. Brown's rooming house and left word with her he'd meet the investors the first of the week at her rooming house.

❋

Monday morning, Jed dressed with more care than usual. He wished to look confident, not desperate, when he pled for financial backing to restock his ranch. Almost six-feet, he buttoned his freshly pressed white shirt, pulled his string tie under his collar, put on a bolo made from an arrowhead he'd found on his ranch, slipped into his rusty suede jacket, and pulled on his Sunday, cream, flat-crowned Mexican hat. He glanced at himself in the mirror and nodded.

He looked down, flicked dust off his rust boots, then tucked the shoe rag into the corner of his bureau drawer.

Jed was totally unaware of the bronzed head to toe picture he presented. His clean-shaven, frosted and wind-burned face matched his look.

"Well, that'll have to do. I have had more profitable times, glad I got these clothes before I got down on my luck," he laughed. *Mother always said, 'No such thing as luck. God controls all, he may let bad things happen, but he's the big boss in the long run.' Wonder what she'd say now if she could see the mess I'm in? I've got to have at least two hundred more cows, but I'd like to have four hundred. Sure going to take a heap of money. She and dad came out of the grasshoppers from Nebraska in 1893 but that didn't kill off all their stock. She said all they had left were peach pits hanging on the bare trees. I thought we had a lot more than that built up, but I lost almost all of it in one blizzard. I've still got friends, seventy five cows and the land, but not much else.*

He rode toward town and a meeting with T.J. Smith.

He considered. *Sure wish I didn't have to do this. I don't like being beholden. Hope this man don't want to tell me what to do. I like being my own boss. Mother's been gone five years and no one has told me what to do since she went on. I know what to do, she sure showed me, but it isn't the same as having someone directing all the time.*

He tied his buckskin in front of a picket fence and

stepped to the porch across the front of Mrs. Brown's rooming house. The door bore a sign, *Let yourself in and ring for assistance.*

Jed obeyed the sign. He twisted his hat in his hand as he awaited a reply to his summons. From where he stood, he heard low feminine voices in the room to his left.

A little man came through the door in the rear of the house.

"May I help you?"

I have an appointment with T. J. Smith?"

The clerk smiled, "Right this way, Sir."

Jed followed the man into the sitting room and looked about. There were no gentlemen in the room. It was occupied only by a pleasant looking woman and a younger woman. Both ladies were dressed in fashionable but dark clothing.

Guess I'm have to wait for him. Sure don't want to talk in front of these ladies. Don't like sitting around, I need to keep moving.

"Right here, Sir," the man directed.

Jed nodded toward the ladies, looked round the room, then sat down in the strongest looking piece of furniture in the whole room, a wing-back chair by the window. He twirled his hat between his big hands. He felt very clumsy and awkward in this feminine room and especially in this chair. Tatted lace items adorned the arms and the back of all the chairs and sofas. A delicate stained glass lamp sat beside his chair on a dainty table.

The clerk smirked and turned to go.

Jed looked up, eager to capture some male presence before the man escaped.

"Sir, I was looking for Mr. Smith, will he be down soon?" Jed asked.

"Not likely," the clerk answered.

"But- I was told to meet T.J. Smith at Mrs. Brown's rooming house."

"Well, that's where you're at and this here's *Miss* T. J. Smith," the clerk motioned toward the younger of the two ladies.

Jed gulped. "You mean- ?" He caught himself before he revealed that he'd expected a man. Jed leaped to his feet.

The clerk barely suppressed his hearty laugh. He coughed as he exited and reached to close the sliding doors pocketed within the walls on either side of the opening. He stiffened his mouth and spoke seriously, "Privacy, I'm sure you'll wish to conduct your business in private. If you need anything, you can summon me with the bell on the side table. Take your time." The two doors clicked in meeting.

The youngest of the two women rose with great dignity. She offered her gloved hand to Jed. He almost dropped his hat, as he shifted it to his left hand.

She clipped into a greeting, "Jed Snowden, your problem has been summarized by Mr. Oliver from the bank. I think we can help each other, if you want to listen to my proposition."

Jed stood speechless at her challenge.

"I assume your silence shows your intention to listen?" she stated.

"Umh- I'm willing to listen, but I don't think- " he managed to grunt.

"Fine, let me lay out my plan for you. My aunt, Mrs. Mary Benton, and myself are in need of a home. In exchange for the restocking of your ranch with between two to four hundred stockers, at my expense, we would expect two sleeping rooms in your ranch house. We'd share kitchen facilities. You'd provide the food, we would do our share of work and help in any way we can. We would not expect to be guests or be waited upon. We're accustomed to taking care of ourselves and taking on other responsibilities."

Jed started to interrupt this diatribe, but he didn't get more than a big breath, before the young woman began again.

"We have three horses and a buggy. We'd require horse pasture and winter hay. We'd need the use of a wagon to haul our furniture and the personal belongings we salvaged from our past residence. Our last home burned. We have only small pieces that won't require much room. Mr. Oliver said you had a two-story ranch house with six rooms. We'd keep these pieces in our bedrooms, we wouldn't clutter your house or crowd you in any way."

Jed felt the air squeezed from his lungs like a collapsed bellows. Before he could suck in a breath, she started again.

"We'd expect to work and keep ourselves occupied. We would not require entertaining. We are decent cooks, can mend and sew, we are quite capable of doing other necessary chores around a homestead, we both ride. Both of us can milk, we know how to garden, and about anything else it takes to make a home run smoothly. However, we would not interfere in the general day to day running of the ranch, unless it appeared to be grossly mismanaged. I'd expect a fair return on my money, the same terms as Mr. Oliver gets at his bank and paid once at the end of each year. The first year, I'd require no payment other than a small allowance of one hundred dollars for our extra personal expenses, because I know the stock won't pay their way for a time." She focused her green eyes directly into Jed's. "Mr. Snowden, do you have any questions?"

She'd caught him out of breath again and with his thoughts scattered.

"Eh, Miss Smith, I'd have to think real hard about this,

but I'll have to be honest with you, if I can find financing elsewhere, I'm inclined to do so."

"Well, Sir, we'll be here two more weeks. If you wish to contract with us, you'll find us here, or Mrs. Brown will know of our whereabouts. Thank you and good day," she gathered her papers.

At her niece's nod, the Mrs. Benton stood to accompany her. The two ladies floated from the room without a backward glance.

Jed sat back down in the chair, totally depleted.

"What was that?" he breathed.

After a few moments of shaking his head, he ran his hand in frustration through his deep auburn curls, gave a shudder and stood on his shaky legs. *Think I'll go back and talk to Mr. Oliver, maybe he'll reconsider.*

He walked from the parlor, opened the front door and stumbled out onto the porch. The bright sunlight blinded him. He failed to see the clerk on the further end of the porch.

A voice sounded to his left, "Been in a whirlwind?"

"What?" Jed asked.

"I asked if you'd been in a whirlwind?" the clerk replied.

"Something, anyway." Jed recovered to ask, "Do you know anything about that young woman and her aunt?"

"Not much. They moved in here a few days ago. They used Banker Oliver as a reference and paid ahead for three weeks lodging." He looked toward the rear of the house, "Mrs. Brown don't like me talkin' 'bout our boarders, so that's all I best say. I just noticed through the window you didn't have much to say."

"No- didn't get much chance." Jed planted his hat on his head, adjusted it firmly and stepped onto the paving stones of the front walk. The buckskin waited patiently, head down, eyes half closed, hip cocked, one hind foot propped, and totally relaxed in the bright sunlight.

The horse came alive at Jed's touch on the stirrup as he rose to his saddle. He looked toward the house and adjusted his hat again. Letting out his breath, he smiled at the clerk.

"You'd better get yourself a storm cellar," the clerk barked a hearty laugh.

"Watch yourself?" Jed replied. He couldn't smile, he felt too unsettled.

He departed when the buckskin's front quarters rose in an immediate easy lope.

❄

Jed spent an uneasy week searching for other means of financing the restocking of his range. Everyone had suffered immense losses in the blizzard. No one had extra cattle, money, or means of acquiring either. He ranged further and further afield, but the blizzard had dissipated generally over the western territories of Kansas, Nebraska, the Dakotas and Texas.

Jed had collected only seventy-five of his own cows. He had, long since, let the two youngest men go. To him, they had seemed relieved and anxious to get somewhere where weather wasn't as harsh, and probably, where they didn't have to work so hard and risk their lives.

They may be the smart ones to get out now.

Jed spoke to his three remaining long-timers, "To restock, I'd have to go east, if I could get far enough away from the path of the blizzard, or over west of the Sangre de Cristo Mountains, or down south toward Mexico."

"Well, you gotta do it," Shaker replied. "You gotta go back and talk to that young gal again. She didn't make too bad a offer."

Jed sighed. "I dread having unrelated females on the place. I can see trouble written all over both of them. That Miss T.J. never took a breath the whole time she talked to me. She sure knew how to give orders and make herself known, she might be that way all the time. What would we do then?"

"I don't know boss, but you could sleep in the bunk house, eat with the boys, like before. You could stay out of their way," Shaker said.

"Yeah, use her money, get on your feet again and then pay her off," Casey added.

Jed scratched below his collar, "If everything went well, it might be not take too many years." He studied his situation, "The terms state I can pay the whole sum ahead of schedule."

"You know she won't want to stay around here long. It'll be too boring for a young lady," Shaker said.

"I've got to make up my mind soon, but I'd rather take a beating than go back there and make that contract with her," Jed said.

"You gotta decide, Boss. We ain't got enough cows to eat off this grass come spring. Time's gettin' short on gettin' 'em moved before calving season," Shaker studied.

"I know. We'd probably have to go hundreds of miles to find stockers," Jed said.

"You could take some men and your horses on the train, then trail a herd back," Max put in.

"Yes, that's about all I can afford right now. I don't want to be any more obligated than I have to. I'll go talk to her Thursday morning. You boys get outfitted. If it works out, we'll take off early next week."

Shaker slapped Casey on the back, "We'll be ready when your financin' is. Right, Max?"

❄

Jed trotted his buckskin into town to make an arrangement with T.J. Smith. When he arrived at Mrs. Brown's Boarding House, the ladies were away. The clerk again led him to the sitting room. The effeminate room left Jed feeling caged.

"Think I'll sit out on the front porch. I'll meet the ladies there and then be on my way. Thank you," Jed waved his hat at the clerk.

❄

Jed twiddled his hat from hand to hand. A half hour passed, then forty five minutes.

If they don't come soon, I'm going to walk down town. Except for my mother, women always make me wait. Lord, give me patience. As much as it's against my better judgement, I've got to get this over.

Jed bowed his head and closed his eyes. *Lord, help me. Let me know what to do.*

The morning was very quiet. Peace settled over him and he dozed. He failed to hear the ladies when they walked up the center of the dirt road.

He roused with a statement from the road.

"Is that the young man who wanted to borrow money from you?" the aunt asked.

The younger woman advanced on Jed, "Mr. Snowden, are you here for our agreement?"

Jed stumbled on the lower step as he quickly rose to greet the women. "Ma'ams," he mumbled. "Yes, if I'm going

to restock, I've got to get to it right away because we'd need
to move the cattle before it gets too late in the spring."

"I'll go to the bank and get your money and the
contract. You'll have to hurry back with the stock before
calving time," T. J. said.

Jed looked down, not wanting her to read his
embarrassment. *I'm surprised a woman is so open about a
cattle operation. Ladies don't usually talk about calving.*

When he looked up, she was on her way toward the
bank. Jed had never seen anyone make up her mind so quickly.
He stood looking after the young woman where she quickly
retreated back toward town.

"Mary Benton," the other woman stuck out her hand,
speaking to him for the first time. "She's a little abrupt. My
brother wanted a boy and he taught her like he would a son.
She can ride and work cattle as good as anyone her age. Her
daddy and mother are both gone and the ranch was too painful
for us to stay on there. I'm very thankful to our Lord that her
mother sold out before the blizzard or we'd be in the same
shape as every other rancher on the Great Plains from Texas
to Canada."

Jed looked at this woman thoroughly for the first time.
*A God-fearing woman, not over forty, knowledgeable, well-
spoken and nice to look at.* "Yes, I'm glad you did get out
before the blizzard. I pity all the poor ranchers and the stock
that suffered through last winter. It almost got me too, but
I've fully recovered my health."

"Were there many citizens lost around here?" she
asked.

"Only four and scattered over a wide area. We had a
couple of hours warning with the winds getting higher by the
minute. Most got into shelter in time. I spent too much time
looking for stock away from our hay ricks. It caught me away

from home, then we were blinded. When I roused, my horse was backed into our windbreak twenty feet from the ranch house. My men helped me recover. We salvaged seventy-five head of our cows and a couple of- uh, others. We lost most of the calves and all the replacement heifers."

"I'm sorry. It was so general, the whole plains suffered incredible losses. I pray we never have another winter like our last," she said.

"Yes, Ma'am, sure hope we never go through anything like that again. It will break this country and all of those now here, if we do. We've already had a couple of bad seasons, but we're due a break soon."

"Most folks can't pull out of this kind of financial loss more than once in a lifetime," she replied.

Jed nodded.

A clerk from the bank arrived with a message from Miss Smith and Banker Oliver.

"Mr. Oliver asks that you come to the bank for the signing of the contract and for him to hand the money directly to you. He doesn't want to be responsible for that kind of transfer on the street."

"I understand," Jed turned, seeking a barrier against the lender. "Mrs. Benton, do you wish to come too?"

"Certainly, don't want to leave T.J. alone in this. You ride ahead, I'll walk over and get there almost as soon as you."

"I'll leave my buckskin and walk with you. I need to stretch my legs, I'm not accustomed to sitting around on porches all day." Jed offered a tight smile.

"I apologize for our absence," Mrs. Benton said.

"I didn't make an appointment. You couldn't have known I would be in town," Jed replied.

"We went down to the church to help for a couple of hours on a quilt for a family who had a burn-out," she explained.

"Good work. I'm sure they will appreciate your effort," Jed said.

After the paper transfer of funds, Jed made an agreement with the banker.

"You give me a couple of hundred cash and a bank draft showing the funds are deposited here and then we'll send a wire to make the transfer once we've made a deal on the cattle. I'll be going east on the train this next week with my men. As soon as we find available stock, we'll be trailing them home.

The banker shifted in his chair, "Yes, that'll be just fine. I'll get my clerk to make out the necessary papers and you can be on your way."

"Thank you." Jed shook his hand.

As the three walked back to Jed's horse, T.J. said, "My aunt and I'll be going along with you to buy the cattle."

Jed stopped short. "What? No, you won't. My men will never tolerate females on a trail drive."

"They will, if *you* tell them," T.J. replied.

"I draw the line here. I'm not telling them and they won't pay any attention to your direction."

"If you don't tell them, I will. Who holds the purse strings in this deal?" she asked.

"I thought you said you wouldn't interfere with the day to day running of the spread?" Jed sputtered.

"I won't be interfering."

Jed slammed his hat on his head and climbed aboard his horse. At the last moment he remembered a detail.

"I'll be sending the wagon in tomorrow for your belongings, if that's all right with you ladies, *Miss T.J. Smith?*"

"That will be just fine, *Sir.*"

Trail Ridin'

Jed moved to the bunk house the day he made arrangements with *Miss* T.J. Smith.

His hands transferred the ladies' belongings from the boarding house to Jed's house the next day. Their move to the ranch was met with curiosity but proved uneventful.

While the ladies settled into their new residence in a couple of the upstairs bedrooms, Jed stayed as far from his house as possible. During several of the next days, the ladies explored and thoroughly cleaning job of the entire house.

True to their word, they stayed out of the business of the hands and Jed.

Trailing cattle wasn't new to Jed's men. They packed their gear, went to town to pick up more cowboys and wrangle horses from other outfits. Within forty-eight hours of the contract, they had their gear and horses ready to go. Shaker had his chuck wagon stocked and ready to hitch up. They would load the wagon on a flat car for transport to the site where it would be needed. The horses and men with their gear would be loaded into freight cars for the trip east.

Jed came into the house to leave a message for the women. T.J. was the only one downstairs.

"We'll be heading out for the east tomorrow, looking for stock cows. I can't leave anyone here to protect you, I need all the men to help move the cows back to the ranch. I think you'll be fine, we haven't had any outlaws come through here for a long while. You assured me you could shoot. There's a rifle over the mantle and here's another."

"You needn't worry about us, *we're going with you*," T.J. stated.

Jed had turned to go, but he spun around, "Surely you're joking?"

"No, I've herded cattle many times. I told you we intend to go along and watch my investment be put to good use. Mary rides too, we've got our horses and had our gear ready for two days. We were beginning to think your men would never be ready to go."

"You're not going," Jed fairly shouted.

"Mr. Snowden, I can stop the use of my money at any time." She clipped her words, "You forget it's still deposited in Mr. Oliver's bank and he agreed to oversee its dispersal. If at any time someone attempted to take advantage of me, I only need to give him the word."

"Well, *I'm* the boss here and *I say you're not going*," Jed huffed.

"Well, *Boss*, did you read your contract before you signed it?" she asked.

"Yes, I did," he growled.

"Well, you'd better look at it again, because *I say* we're going and we are," she said.

"You can't!"

"What time are *we* leaving in the morning?" T.J. asked sweetly.

Jed turned on his heel and stomped from the house.

I'm so angry I'm afraid of what I might say. Lord, give me the words and the patience to deal with this woman. Who does she think she is anyway, the boss? In no way is she going to take over here. I can't let her. The men would laugh me off this range if they knew I gave in to her. Help me!

T.J. tramped upstairs, "Mary, get your saddle out of your trunk and let's finish up. We're leaving in the morning to buy the cattle."

"What time?" Mary asked.

"I couldn't get that out of him. He's too stubborn. We'll get up very early and when the men come from the bunk house, we'll be in the saddle and loaded up," she directed.

"Good thing you got the horses reshod last week. Know how far we'll have to ride?" Mary asked.

"No, *the boss* said we're going east on the train until we locate cattle for sale. Then we'll trail them home."

Mary touched her finger to her lip, "Better put in plenty of jerky and hardtack. Let's load up a side of bacon and some beans too. Grub may be hard to come by if we're far from towns. I saw Shaker's chuck wagon come in with supplies but they may not have figured on two extra hands to feed."

"We may end up feeding the men too, so best be a little extra prepared," T.J. stated.

Mary looked closely at T.J.'s face. "Did he really say we could go?"

"No."

"Well, that was short and sweet. Are you sure we are going?"

"Yes. Like I said, we'll be out front between the house and the trail and be prepared. He won't want a scene in front of his hands. He'll knuckle under. Besides, I told him to re-read his contract. He doesn't have a choice," T.J. asserted.

"Theodosia Jesse, I hope you don't overstep someday and get us both in trouble."

"Aunt Mary, don't call me that! You know I don't like that name."

"I know young lady, but I have to make you think like a lady once in a while."

"Please get packed, let's not talk about it anymore. We need to get to bed right away or we'll have trouble getting up in the morning in time to pull off our little trip."

"Just as you say, *you're the boss*," Mary snickered.

❄

Jed stepped into the bunk house. The men were settling for the night.

"We'll leave the ranch at four in the morning. Do whatever you need to do tonight, or get up early enough to get it accomplished. We've got our horses ready and in the corral. They got a good feed tonight. We've got grain and our grub on Shaker's wagon. We'll be traveling light, just like we said. Take what you personally need behind your saddle in your bedroll. If you forget something, you'll do without. We'll probably be gone close to a month, maybe longer. Do you have any questions?"he asked.

"Wake me as soon as you get up, I'm a heavy sleeper," Max said.

"Fine. Besides waking you up, let's keep the noise down in the morning. No sense in waking the dead when we leave. Good night boys." Jed turned sharply on his heel and went to his own bunk. He gathered his belongings into a bedroll, then placed it at the foot of his bunk in readiness.

Neither T.J. nor Mary slept well. When Mary's mantle clock struck the half hour after two, they arose quietly.

When she was dressed, Mary led their three horses from their stalls, out the back door of the barn and took them to the hitching rail off the porch at the front of the main house. The two saddled, tied their bedroll gear, grub bag and slickers behind their saddles. Each carried an additional bag in front of their saddles. The spare animal they loaded with additional food and camp gear.

Mary spoke quietly, "I heard that clock strike every time last night."

"Me too," T.J. whispered.

They resumed their quiet wait.

When the hands rounded the shadowed ranch house, they saw two additional young men astride their horses and a pack horse on lead.

Shaker spoke first, "Boss, didn't know you hired on those extras?"

"We'll see about them," Jed clipped off his words in a quiet voice. "Wait here, I'll be right back and we'll move out." He lifted his reins, touched his horse with a smooth spur and clucked the animal forward between the two.

"What do you think you're doing?" he asked.

"I told you we were going. I'm very honest. One of these days, you'll learn I mean what I say," T.J. said in a low voice.

He turned to reason with the older woman. "Mrs. Benton, do you understand what your niece means to do?"

"Yes, we wouldn't be out here in men's clothing if we weren't prepared to carry through on her proposal," she said.

Jed puffed in resignation, "I can't stop you from tagging along, short of tying you both up, but don't expect any concessions to be made. We've got hard work to be done."

"We know that, we've been on drives before," T.J. huffed back at him.

"Where you sleep out and go for days without changing your clothes, or taking a bath?" Jed asked.

"Yes, you'll find we can get as dirty as the next cowhand," T.J. said.

"You will," Jed rubbed the back of his neck. "We rotate positions, you'll take your turn at drag and night herd, just like the rest of the *cowboys*."

"Fine. Hadn't we better move on?" T.J. asked.

Impertinent! Irritated, Jed fisted his hand on the reins. *Lord, what do I do now?* He checked his reins hard to the right and turned aside. He reached down to pat his horse on the neck to make amends. *I never mean to be harsh, but I regret taking it out on my buckskin.* "Good girl." The animal flicked back an ear to catch the soft words. Then her attention diverted to the road ahead.

The two ladies fell in behind the following hands.

The hands were confused and mumbled together as they rode.

"When and where did he get them two?" Max asked.

"They look like kids, bet they're green hands," Casey said.

"Don't know. Somehow them horses look familiar," Shaker ruminated.

"Too dark to tell, maybe by daylight we'll see someone we know," Max said.

"Kinda hate to be out with extra strangers on a drive. Got to depend on each other too much to have someone irresponsible with us," Casey said.

"Well, the boss ain't steered us wrong yet. Guess we'll wait and see," Shaker replied. "We got plenty of grub and a job to do. Let's get at it and hope we find some good cows or we'll all be out of jobs."

A jolly silence fell on the sleepy hands.

Alone, the boss rode stiff and seething at the front of the band. *Warm, I am plumb hot!*

The pair at the rear dropped back a few yards and moved in silent companionship for miles.

Breaking the silence, Mary commented, "I congratulate you."

"Why?" T.J. asked.

"You accomplished our goal without a big civil war," Mary explained.

"He's an agreeable man, just got to handle him right," T.J. replied smugly.

"I hope you really do know what you're doing, but if I were you, I'd watch my step. Get too cocky and you may get your tail feathers yanked," Mary warned.

"I don't intend to be cocky, we'll do a great job and no one will be able to find anything wrong with our work. Real cowhands don't complain if everyone pulls his own load."

"Hope so, missy. Sometimes I think you've got a lot to learn about men. They're not quite as easy to steer as you would like to believe. One of these days, you are going to meet your match and then watch out!"

"Daddy always- "

"*Daddies* don't count, they're real suckers when it comes to their little girls," Mary said.

"That's the way I always found it at home with the hands. I can hold my own," T.J. said.

"Being on your daddy's ranch might have made a difference you know. You just might have gotten some special treatment out of those hands. I remember when you first started going along with my brother. The hands thought it was cute for a little girl to be so capable on a horse. They let you get by with much that a boy might not have been able to get away with."

"I did everything I was able to do for my size and strength. They never let me off easy," T.J. argued.

"I don't know about that. Didn't you ever see old Dud get ahead of some of your cows, or Luke smack that old bull that threatened you? Don't you remember that kid cowboy blowing the head off that rattler a foot in front of you? They watched out for you, but maybe you were too much of a kid to see it. I noticed though. So did Roy and your daddy. He appreciated what the men did for you. Most of them would have risked their life for you, or him."

"I know. I did appreciate it then, but I miss them now."

They rode in silence.

A few miles further, T.J. spoke, "More than the hands, I miss Daddy," she sighed.

"Me too. He was a good brother, husband- father. Too bad the good sometimes die young."

"Mother didn't last to be very old either," T.J. added.

"No, another of the same, but she didn't have the strength to run the ranch after your daddy died. Roy and I were too far away to be around all the time. Things started going downhill, then she got sick. Arranging to sell the ranch was very hard, but it was the best thing she could have done for you. You had to go along with the sale. It all came out for the best with the blizzard coming on so soon."

"Yes. Then Roy was gone and you came to take care of me after mother died. Aunt Mary, I do appreciate all you've done for me." T.J. turned to look at her aunt, "Why didn't you have children of your own?"

"Guess the good Lord knew I'd be needed somewhere else. Me and Roy wanted a family, it just never happened. Don't know why, we both seemed healthy enough. We worked hard and time drifted along, then he was gone and there hasn't been anyone since."

"Do you ever regret not having your own family?" T.J. questioned.

"I miss Roy, wish he was back, but you're my family and have been for a long while. I'm happy enough. How about you, are you really happy?" Mary asked.

"Sometimes I don't know. I get kind of restless, there isn't always a reason I can put my finger on," the young woman said.

"I expect you'll want a family of your own one of these days, then I'll move on to something else,"Mary said.

"Mary, I don't want you to leave. You got to be my-*sister* a long time ago. I'll never outgrow needing you."

"I hope not, but you will find your own, then you won't need me in the same way."

T.J. looked down. "Are you looking for another love?"

"I don't know, child. Sometimes I have a stirring of interest, but so far, that stirring hasn't led anywhere. Who knows? We'll live one day at a time, relying on the Lord to see us through and provide what we need the most. I can ask you the same thing. You looking, got your eyes open?"

"Sure, but I haven't been bitten yet by an all consuming interest in any one man. Maybe some day. Who knows?" T.J. questioned.

"Make him a Christian man, Honey. Won't no other kind do for you."

"You ever think about what you'd want in another man?" T.J. asked.

"He'd have to be a Christian, strong like Roy. He doesn't have to be handsome as Roy, but that don't hurt either. What do you want T.J.?"

"He's got to be strong in every way, including following the Lord. I guess he's got to be stronger than me."

"Is that possible?" Mary asked.

"Yes, if I wanted it to be."

"Keep praying, the Lord will provide," Mary said.

By the time the cowhands had ridden the ten miles to town, rosy streaks of daylight broke over the eastern horizon. Jed led his crew through town.

They dismounted and stretched their legs.

Jed stood leaning against his buckskin. *I mean to play T.J.'s game as long as it takes for the men to identify the intruders, then I'll watch for the outcome. Hope I can send them back real soon.*

They watered their animals then turned east and journeyed on toward the railhead.

Miles passed uneventfully. A day passed, then into the second. The crew ate along the trail from their packs.

Occasionally one or another dropped out for a short time or to stretch their legs. Saddles were changed from horse to horse to enable a balancing of the work load among the stock. They herded or led their loose horses along between the groups.

Shaker looked at the boss. "What do you 'spose is eatin' him? He ain't hisself this trip."

"Guess he's just worried about finding the stock and all the money it'll take to get what he needs," Max said.

"I guess. *Big responsibility, bi-ig responsibility.*"

❈

The crew loaded aboard a stock car with hay on the floor. Their horses occupied a separate car and the chuck wagon one end of a flat car.

As the train got underway, the two green hands lounged quietly or slept in a dark corner.

The regular crew jawed and played cards near the light of the open door.

"They sure ain't friendly," Shaker said.

"Maybe they're just shy. Probably never been away from home before," Max surmised.

Jed leaned on the door jamb on the other side of the car.

"What's wrong with the boss?" Casey asked.

"Must have a burr under his saddle. He ain't told us," Shaker said.

On the third afternoon's break, Shaker's head came around. He watched the familiar horse the smallest man led from the water trough. He looked again at the youth as he passed, then directly into the man's face.

He gasped, "Miss T.J., what are you doin' here?"

"Same thing you are."

For once, Shaker was caught speechless. He stopped to watch the young woman, then took a second look at the other stranger. *Same deal, them women been along all the time. No wonder they hung back and didn't mix with the other hands.*

He couldn't wait to tell the other hands. The hands moved to the stream. When the two smaller hands moved away and began to walk to load, Shaker spoke to the other men.

"Now I think I know why the boss has been so upset."

"How's that?" Casey asked.

"Did you take a good look at them two young fellars that hang to the corner?"

"Not really, too dark at night and during the early mornings in the stock car. They hang back and don't mix when we get out, figured they was bashful or unfriendly. Why?" Max asked.

"Them two young fellars, ain't fellars," Shaker said.

"Come on. Who'd be taking anyone but fellows on a trail drive?" Max asked.

"Shaker, sometimes you are a windy one," Casey laughed.

The other new men kept quiet and listened.

"No, take a look at them two horses. Ever seen 'em before?" Shaker asked.

"Maybe, but I can't rightly think just where." Casey rubbed his stubbled cheeks.

"How about in our own pasture and corrals, maybe in our barn?" Shaker asked.

"Yeah, they might be some of ours, guess the boss has

to lend them some horses. That ain't so unusual."

"No it ain't. More'n half of the ones we brought along belong to the boss."

"You ever seen that sorrel hooked to Mrs. Benton's buggy, or that bay following along behind?" Shaker asked.

"Yes, you might be right. But how come the boss brought along Miss T.J. and Mrs. Benton's horses? They might need them while we're gone," Casey said.

"Ever' ranch is short a horses after last winter. Didn't too many of ours make it through," Max added.

"You're all thick as eight by eights. Who's them young men leading them horses?" Shaker scoffed.

"We said we didn't know them when they met us that first morning. I still don't," Max said.

"Nope, never seen 'em before," Casey replied.

"How 'bout if they wasn't young men?" Shaker asked.

"A woman? Couldn't be. Women don't wear pants and ride like that."

"Some do and these two shur do," Shaker replied.

"Come on Shaker. Your eyesight must be gettin' dim in your old age," Max said.

"Look again. I think it's your eyesight, or your brains one," Shaker scoffed.

"Okay, we give up, who are they?" Casey asked.

Shaker shook his head. "Didn't think I'd have to draw you a picture in the dust. Them's Miss T.J. and Mrs. Benton. Take a look for yourself if you don't believe me."

"Well, I sure will, can't believe you'd joke us this way, Shaker. This is way below your usual style," Casey said.

"Well, you blamed fools, I ain't gonna take this kind of

talk from you. If you're so dumb, just find out for yourselves." Shaker pulled his hat down until it jammed his ears, then stalked off leading two horses behind him.

"What a joke. That ole geezer tried a good one on us this time," Max laughed.

"You know, he might be right. Look at that little 'un. Don't he walk kind of short-stepped for a boy?" Casey asked.

"Might, but how would they ride with us for all this time and keep that kind of secret?"Max asked.

"Don't know, but them two already done a few things that I didn't expect," Casey said.

"Guess you might be right, but I aim to take a good look at 'em when we get loaded back up," Max said.

"There's the boss' signal, you ain't gonna have to wait long," Casey signaled.

The four hands stood back, first on one foot and then the other when the two women hurried back to the loading chute.

"Auntie, I think we been found out," T.J. grinned.

"Think you're right. Did you see them standing there all so polite and staring like we were something strange?" Mary stated.

"I guess we are something strange. Women dressed like men and riding astride, don't see that very often, unless it's on a woman's own ranch, then not usually in front of other men than her husband," T.J. commented.

"Or an Indian woman," Mary said.

"Yes, I think we kind of scared them good this time," T.J. smirked.

"I want to see how this turns out and how they act

now," Mary said.

"Me too. They wouldn't dare touch us, but it's going to be a bit strained." T.J. said.

"Bet their language will be cleaned up a bit." Mary grinned.

"Daddy wouldn't have let us bet, but you're right there, T.J. smirked.

Cattle Buying

A few days later, Jed broke his brooding silence. "Keep your eyes open. When you start seeing herds of cattle, call out. We'll unload and spread out, see what we can find. We'll stay south of the Missouri River so we won't have to swim them across."

A day later, they found their bonanza in western Missouri, pastured in the lush river hills.

"You think there's enough here to make it worth our while?" Shaker asked the boss.

"Guess we better try. It looks promising. We'd be this much closer to home if we don't go further east. We can buy what we can find, pen them at the railroad pens for a few days until we can make up our herd."

"These don't look much like western cows. Can they take the weather?"

Jed looked at the herd. "Where do you think some of them western cattle came from?"

"Some from here, but most from Mexico."

"Yes, we'll have to do some cross-breeding, but this won't be a big herd and maybe the good Lord will give us a few mild winters to get them toughened. Guess we'll find out," Jed stated.

Jed spoke to the hands. "Get your gear together. Every two of you will go out looking for cattle. Take along a pack animal with some grub. When you find a likely herd, come back to our main camp and I'll go see what we can buy."

"Shaker, you go with Mrs. Benton and Miss T.J."

Shaker looked startled. He huffed, "Boss-

Jed shook his head.

Everyone scrambled to be loaded and ready. The group together had become less boring when they discovered the two ladies amongst their crew, but their train car quarters grew smaller every day.

The settled areas of Missouri seemed more confining to them than their open spaces of Jed's western ranch.

Jed managed to find fifty head of cows between two partners near Lexington, Missouri. He was directed to another farmer who had thirty he'd sell.

Shaker and the ladies found twenty five more. They ran the cows into a trail pen, a small herd at a time. The hands all leaned on the top rail of the fence to watch the cows fight. Each new herd brought another uproar.

"Guess they'll get their pecking order established and settle down by the time we get the bunch together," Jed said.

T.J. leaned next to Jed. "I certainly hope so. I don't want to see any of these animals crippled. Wish that old black cow had her horns cropped. She's a mean one."

"We can't rope her now, she's too close to dropping her calf," Jed observed.

"No, guess not. Maybe we'll make it home with her

before she rips up one of the other cows," T.J. said.

"What about those two b-, gentleman cows?" Shaker asked.

"I think that little one will give it up before long, then he'll stay out of the old fellow's way," Jed replied.

"This pen's kind of small. Guess we could build another one," T.J. added.

"They got to get over it sometime, might as well be now as on the trail," Jed replied.

"Yes, but on the range there's much more space, there they can each have their own territory. If we don't keep them healthy, they won't have that opportunity," T.J. said.

By the next morning, the first of their cattle had made a shaky peace. The crew fanned out again for more cow buying expeditions.

Over the next few days, the herd grew until they had three hundred and eighty-seven cows and ten bulls scattered over several areas.

Jed met the crew after supper that night.

"Shaker, get the grub together first thing in the morning, then head along the river toward Kansas. You can pick up fresh supplies at the best town on your route. Tonight, divide up the grub we got left between the hands." He looked around the circle.

"We'll line them out at daylight in the morning. Shaker, you'll be able to travel faster than we can. Settle in at a good camp ground or at another railroad pen the right distance and we'll be along as soon as we can." Jed looked at the other crew members, "Tomorrow's gonna be a rough day, these cattle aren't trail broke and we'll have to work extra hard. We'll only go a few miles the first day or so, but I hope we get back to the

ranch before we gain any little doggies. Get some sleep except
for the night watch. This may be the last day with a fence.
Take advantage of this last easy night."

Excitement rippled through the crew. The night guard
broke out his saddle. When ready, he climbed aboard for the
first shift at night herd. The others took their saddle and
blanket, then rolled up around the campfire. T.J. and Mary
rolled up on the western outskirts of the group.

After several hours T.J. whispered, "Mary, can you
sleep?"

"No, but I'm trying to."

"Be morning soon, I can't wait to get on the trail."

"It'll be here soon enough, don't wish for it. By tonight,
we're gong to wish for a longer night," Mary whispered.

"Guess you're right. Hope I can sleep a few more
minutes." T.J. smoothed the blanket under her head.

Made up of a well-trained crew, the hands functioned
well the next day. Only the stock was at odds as to what was
expected. Some continually turned back, wishing to return to
their previous homes. Others lagged and had to be prodded
along. Confusion reigned.

T.J. and Mary, from their left flank positions,
continually brought animals back into the line.

In passing close to each other, T.J. spoke, "I'm glad we
don't have the drag. Those fellows are really doing the hard
work today."

"Yes, I think Jed put his most experienced men back
there on the best horses. Did you notice he's right in the middle
of the tail of this bunch?"

"Yes, he usually takes the hardest jobs himself," T.J. noted.

"You have to admire him for that," Mary said.

"Yes, I give him trouble, but he is an admirable person," T.J. added.

"He isn't half bad to look at either," Mary added.

"Are you staking a claim?" T.J. asked.

"No, I'm too old for him, but you might take another look."

"I have, but I don't want to mix business with my personal life."

"You might consider it. He's a Christian; he's got character; you both like ranching. You'd make a good pair with your money and his land. You like his part of the country. It could be a going business *and* personal relationship."

"You forgot one thing."

"What's that?" Mary asked.

"I don't love him," T.J. said.

"I'd expect that to come along. Wouldn't be good to marry without love. I know that from past experience."

"I know you loved Roy, but you don't talk much about your marriage."

"I didn't love him when we first married. I didn't really know him, but he was a fine man and we grew to love each other very much. We had a good seven years together. I enjoyed being with him. He was a good friend. We liked to work side by side."

T.J. looked at her aunt. She saw a wistful, far-away look on the other woman's face. A pang of loneliness snaked through T.J.'s chest.

A cow darted off to the south and T.J. left to retrieve her.

After a week on the trail, the cows lined out and the work became easier for the hands.

Another few days and T.J. dropped behind the drive when a cow loitered. The cow lay down, then arose with the obvious signs of imminent birth of their first calf.

After a couple of hours and with no difficulty in the birth, the old cow allowed the little one to suckle while nervously eyeing T.J.

Two hours after the herd moved on, T.J. led her horse between the cow and her still damp calf.

"Okay, sister, about time we hit the trail." She dropped the bridle reins and attempted to lift the calf in front of her saddle. Halfway up the side of her horse, she realized the task was beyond her strength. She turned to look over possible solutions to her problem.

She crowded the calf along toward a ditch. The cow threatened T.J.

"If you don't let me help you move your calf, we'll never catch up. Don't you know I have to do this? You two can't stay out here by yourselves. There might be wolves and other critters that would make a quick meal of this little one."

T.J. heaved the calf up into her arms. It let out a tiny bawl.

With incensed maternal instincts, the cow made a jump for the girl.

"Get out of here!" T.J. struck at the cow with her hat, while she tried to hold the calf with her other arm. They both went down backwards against her mare. The horse shifted

The cow bellowed, foam dripped from her open mouth and she bounced again. The girl shoved the calf toward its mother and made her escape under the horse's belly. She came up on the far side.

"Need some help?" a masculine voice sounded.

T.J.'s heart jerked, she lurched against her horse and turned her head.

"Jed?"

"Missed a hand, rode back to see what was the problem. Been watching you as I rode in. You did a good job, but I think now's a good time to call on your partner for a little assistance. You get aboard, ride between the cow and that calf and I'll toss it on my horse while you keep her busy."

Jed rode between the cow and T.J.'s horse while he spoke.

"You can get on, she's corralled for a minute and busy with this little girl."

T.J.'s hands were wet and slippery. In her first reach, her hand slipped off the saddle horn to jerk her off balance. She caught herself with her horse's mane. She grabbed a handful and bounced again on her right foot. Upright in her saddle, she reached down for her forgotten reins. To herself, she thought, *Fool, put on a real show like you never rode a horse before. Between the cow and the boss, I'm plumb flustered.*

She looked quickly at Jed, but he was occupied with the irate cow. *Good, he didn't see that blunder and my slip.*

"Okay, I'll cross this ditch and move the old cow. Are you ready?" T.J. asked.

"Have at it. As soon as you're over here, I'll grab this calf," Jed said.

T.J. moved her horse between the cow and the calf. The baby nosed the mare, thinking anything with legs was her mother. The woman was distracted between the cow and the calf, but when the cow bawled, she turned her full attention to diverting the surly mother. She heard a grunt.

"All right, I'm aboard with our first addition, let's start back. You might follow her. As soon as she gets wind of her calf, she'll follow, but she may be confused for a minute," Jed said.

Several times the old cow attempted to return to the birthing site to recover her calf, but each time T.J. and Bess won out and moved her along after Jed. The calf bawled and the cow lined out to follow where Jed rode with his little burden across his lap. The calf's legs hung off over either of his thighs.

After a few minutes, T.J. wiped her hands down the sides of her trousers, pushed a few stray strands of hair up under her hat and congratulated herself on a good job, with no one hurt. Her congratulatory silence was interrupted by a question from Jed. She didn't catch his intent.

"What did you say?" she asked.

"I said, why don't you ride up here, so we can discuss how we're going to handle this addition? That old cow knows where her little one is now, so she'll keep up."

"What do you have in mind?" she asked.

"I was thinking, I've seen calves slung over a pack horse with their hind feet in a grub bag. If they're balanced heavy on the hind quarters, they'll stay put for a long while after they get a little tired. We may have to let this calf walk a few miles every day first though.

"Sounds like a good idea, or I can pack her," T.J. offered.

"Hard to work safely with a calf to manage. I think the pack horse idea is a better one," Jed reasoned.

"She sure won't be able to walk far. I've seen the little fellows streaming foam with their mouths open and all tuckered. Soon they start to stagger, plus the problem with worried cows trampling them."

Jed commented absent mindedly, "Real trail-herders kill all the calves, but our object is to restock my range. I can't waste a year getting another calf out of this ole cow. Gotta take care of this one."

T.J. bristled, "No, I'd work very hard before I'd let you kill this baby." She gave Jed a hard, searching look.

"Don't look like that. I never killed a trail calf in my life, unless he was a whole lot older and the crew needed fresh meat."

"I kind of hoped you hadn't made a habit of disposing of young animals," she said.

"There's the dust from the herd, we'll be up on them before you know it. I'll ride on up when we catch the tail enders and you can settle back into your position. I'll pick up a pack horse and get this little one settled," Jed commented.

"You may have to bring her back to the rear. I think the whole herd will confuse this cow and the fresh birth smell may set them off," she said.

"You're right. If she won't go up on the side of the herd, I'll come back and set this calf down at the rear. Then I'll go get the pack animal while you keep an eye on the pair," he said.

"Fine," T.J. said.

That settled, they rode on in companionable silence.

Away from the dust of the herd, T.J. admired the scenery, then turned to admire the damp swirls of hair on the calf's head. Before she realized it, her gaze moved up to the damp auburn curls on Jed's forehead, where his hat was shoved back from his lighter forehead. Her gaze moved to his eyes. He looked straight at her.

T.J. dropped her eyes to her hands, as her cheeks flamed with embarrassment.

Jed didn't look away from her down turned face.

A few green blades began to show through the dry stems of winter. Hungered for fresh forage, the cows grabbed at blades as they passed. Each mouthful delayed the herd. Tempers shortened.

That night, fire lit the sky. The air freshened and the wind rose. A slashing rain began.

The hands pulled their slickers from their packs and moved restlessly in their bed rolls.

T.J. and Mary rose to shove the calf under Shaker's wagon. The cow hunched in the lee of the wagon and turned her rump to the rain.

Jed saddled and rode out to the night herders. As he met each of the men, he spoke quietly, "Keep an eye out. We could get a lightning strike or a stampede if this doesn't blow over soon."

He continued his instructions, "Get some soothing noise going to keep them from startling from any little thing."

The men moved off singing in an easily heard but soothing manner. The lightning distanced and moved away.

"I see a few stars, think we got by this time," T.J. whispered to Mary.

"Catch another nap, it will be time to get started sooner than we want."

Time was running out. The first calf was joined by a mate, then another, and another, bringing further delays.

T.J. rode near where Jed looked over their situation.

"Why don't you and the boys ride on ahead? Leave one man with my aunt and I. We'll bring these little fellows along at their own speed."

"I'd hate to do that, it might not be safe," Jed said.

T.J. paid no attention to his objection. "You could cut out a few of the heavier cows and leave them too."

He looked at the cows slowed by the calves and the two smallest on the pack horses.

She argued further, "As soon as you get home, you could send back a wagon and a few of the men to help us along."

"I wouldn't want to leave you alone out here," Jed said.

"We wouldn't be alone with one of the men along. Mary and I each have a pistol."

"You have pistols?" Jed asked.

"And we know how to use them too," She didn't wait for his comment. "You could leave Shaker's saddle scabbard and his rifle. Then if several more cows calve along our route, you could let another hand drop out to tend those. We'd catch up in a day or so. I doubt we'd be far behind."

"I'll have to think about it." He rode on ahead abruptly.

That afternoon, Jed saw the two youngest cowpokes start away from the herd. He rode after them.

When he came up to them, they had a coyote stretched

out between them at the ends of their ropes. The two had managed to rope the animal.

"Fellows, if they're close enough to bother the calves and to catch in an easy way, that's all right, but don't use up these horses. They had too hard a winter and we're not home yet."

The two looked sheepish.

"This 'un been trying for a weak calf," one of the young men replied.

"You can get rid of it, but don't rope anymore."

While Jed was out of the herd's sight, he looked back toward the dust from the drag.

I've studied on it. I can't leave T.J. and Mary. What if something happened? I'd never forgive myself. He looked off toward home, then turned his horse and made a complete circle. *Pretty tame country- few coyotes of the four legged variety have been following the herd; don't know about the two legged kind. Cattle are in short supply all around, someone might decide he needs ours. Can't leave the ladies, I can't do it! I'd be worried about T.J. and the others.*

Three days and ten more calves, he no longer had a choice. They used all the loose horses for calf packers, but the pace was far too slow.

"Boys, I've made a decision. Max, you'll be in charge of the drive of the main herd. We'll cut out the cows heaviest with calf. The ladies and I will stay behind and bring up the stragglers and their calves. If any more calves drop in the main drive, you'll take them along until there are more than you can handle. Then you'll leave a few hands with that bunch and we'll catch up as soon as we can." Jed continued, "When you get the balance of the herd settled on home range, leave two men there. Bring a wagon with side boards and return to help move the slowest animals toward home. We have an unusual situation going for us here. We have to adjust to handle it. I'm sure you know we will need every one of these calves to restock. We can't afford to lose them. We'll try to give them the best care we can here on the trail."

Jed looked at each of the hands. "Do you fellows have any other suggestions, or thoughts?" he asked.

The ladies stayed quiet, the men shifted uneasily.

"All right, that's the plan for tomorrow. Everyone, thank you for your faithfulness thus far. Remember I'm counting on all of you to carry on whether I'm with you or elsewhere. Casey and Max, you've got the first watch. Everyone else, get a good night's rest."

The hands quickly dispersed to their duties or bed rolls.

T.J. and Mary rolled into their blankets nearest the calves.

T.J. was in the midst of a dream when someone shook her shoulder.

"Miss? We got a problem-   can you come?" Jed asked softly.

She was on her feet before coming fully awake. She staggered against the man who had awakened her.

"Sorry, can't seem to get my feet awake."

"That's all right. We got a cow having a problem. Our hands are too big. Have you ever turned a calf?" he asked.

"I've helped."   *

"T.J. what's the matter?" Mary asked.

"Mary, there's a calving problem," T.J. said.

"I'll be right there," Mary said.

They approached a down cow that moaned as she strained.

"Think you can handle this one?" Jed asked.

T.J. shoved up her sleeve and wiped lard from Shaker's cooking supply on her exposed arm.

Jed held a flaming torch for light.

"I don't see anything," Mary commented.

"All right, be sure she stays still," T.J. directed.

Max kneeled on the cow's neck. T.J. knelt and began to feel in the birth canal with her fingers. All she could feel was a furry hide. She moved her fingers left, then right.

"I think I've got it figured out. The neck is there with the head turned back. I don't find any feet. I think we need to shove it back and then untangle everything." She shoved with all her might, then again. "I can't budge it." She motioned to Jed, "We can do this. Put your knee on my elbow and shove when I say to."

"Don't let me hurt you," Jed cautioned.

"I'll tell you if you're shoving too hard," T.J. said.

Steady pressure was applied to T.J.'s elbow as she shoved against the neck of the calf with the heel of her hand. "It's moving. I can feel it give. Now I've got some room."

Jed let off the pressure on her elbow.

"Here's a foot and another. I always wonder if they're front or back," she said.

"It won't matter, if you've got two of the same end, but once we start, if it's breech, we'll have to move fast, or we'll lose the calf."

"Let me go up to the knees and I think I'll be able to tell. A bump in front, this is a front one. This one's bent back, that's a front one too. Now to get the nose started. All right, I'm going to come out, get a piece of that twine ready," T.J. directed.

Mary handed T.J. the heavily twisted twine. "I've made a loop in the end."

"Here goes. I got both feet looped. Now, pull a little. Wait, let me get this nose started better. This calf is alive, it's sucking my fingers."

T.J. put her fingers into the nostrils and moved the head into position over the front knees. "There, think it's all set, pull again."

The cow moaned with each pull and renewed her efforts.

"Great, it's coming. I think I can take my hand off the nose now. Keep a steady tension, I think we've got it with the cow's assistance."

Two little hooves appeared, then a pink nose, then over the eyes. Jed and Mary continued their steady pull. Now the ears became visible, one more mighty heave and the little heifer slid free. The cow gathered her hind feet under her, suddenly very interested in her new delivery.

Jed pulled T.J. against him and away from the cow. Her legs were unsteady from the kneeling, she leaned against him for a moment.

Mary made one last swipe at the little heifer's nose and stepped back from the possessive cow.

"I never cease to marvel when that happens. God has such a marvelous creation, but sometimes he needs our help to make it all come about on schedule. I'm thankful he lets us have that part, but it's not always such a good ending," Mary said.

Jed stepped back to T.J. and Mary's side, listening to the ladies' comments.

" 'In travail, she shall bring forth her first born.' This really isn't her first born, but somewhere down the line," T.J. added her thought from the Bible.

"She's yours," Jed stated. *She's good help.*

"What do you mean?" T.J. asked.

"Miss T.J., she's yours. You saved her, she's yours. Start your own herd, whatever you want."

"I'm grateful, but I really can't take her. You'll need all you've got to make a go of this. Just give me the yearly allowance and make payments. That will get you paid up and free all that much quicker," she said.

Jed's voice came out gruff, "Why can't you?"

"I'm sorry, but I can't accept her as a gift."

"She's not a gift, you earned her," Jed threw the burning torch toward the fire and turned on his heel, he stalked back toward the bedrolls.

"He can't give the calves to all the hands, he'd never get started," she said.

The two women's eyes adjusted quickly to the returned darkness. They sat near the new mother and her calf

"Look how she always licks upward. She almost picks her calf up with her tongue," T.J. observed.

They saw the little animal stagger up and make tentative efforts to nurse. The human task was finished.

Mary spoke, "Theodosia, I think you owe that man an apology. He made a gesture and you knocked him down flat."

"How can you say that?" T.J. protested.

"He was genuinely grateful. He hasn't been able to do anything for you to pay for the good work you've done.

Giving the little heifer to you made up for some of that, but you weren't gracious in your rejection of his efforts. Plus you took away his manly pride. That's a very fragile and precious thing to a man, it's also the way a woman can hurt him quicker than any other way."

"Surely not," came T.J.'s casual answer.

"T.J., think about it. You'll understand what I mean. Just wait and see if he isn't a little stand-offish in the morning."

"Oh, Mary, you make things too complicated. Don't be so serious about every little thing."

"Some things that seem silly to us women, are very serious to men. Their ego is the most fragile thing they have. Watch your step you don't bruise it so brutally."

"Mary! Go to sleep," T.J. whispered.

T.J. lay awake a long while. *I didn't mean to offend his fragile male ego. Daddy always said I had a quick tongue. Guess I'd better bridle it. What a mess, can't say what I think without hurting someone's feelings. I didn't mean anything bad by my refusal. Stupid men, I was just trying to help him out.* She turned over. *No, he's not stupid, what a silly thing for me to say. Lord, guess I'd better ask your and his forgiveness. Please make life more simple, I'm too tired to think about all this now.* She hit her blanket to remove a bump that troubled her.

T.J. slept a little longer than usual the next morning. She'd been awake too long last night between the delivery of the calf and her thoughts on her own misdeeds.

The main herd drifted away before she jolted awake to see the cows grazing quietly. The older calves played tag with their tails over their backs.

She laughed, "Don't worry, you fellows will be tired in a couple of hours and then beg us to haul you."

"Miss T.J., you going with us this morning?"

She turned to see Jed astride his buckskin, ready to start the cows and calves on their way following the distant dust of the larger herd.

She scrambled up, "Mr. Snowden, I'm truly sorry for my refusal of your gift last night. Please don't think I'm ungrateful for your offer, but I thought I was doing what was best for the ranch. I was trying to help you out."

Formal, Jed answered, "Miss T.J., you have helped immensely, I thank you." He pulled the rein of his horse and turned away.

She hastily rolled her bedroll and put her belongings on the back of her saddle. Her mare stood, mysteriously saddled and ready. She looked around. Mary was no where in sight.

"Who saddled this horse?" No one answered, because only the horse was within hearing distance.

"Mary, did you saddle my horse this morning?"

"No, but I saw who did."

They rode on in silence for a few moments. T.J. fidgeted.

"Who?" she asked.

"Who, what?" Mary asked.

"You know, who saddled my horse this morning?"

"The Boss."

"Oh no, I overslept. I'm totally embarrassed. I told him we'd never hold him up on this drive or need to be taken care of."

Mary threw up her hands, "T.J., do you never learn? I told you he wanted to do something to thank you. Now you're embarrassed and upset because he did do something for you. Let him thank you, ple-ease."

"I'll have to find someway to thank him back," T.J. lamented.

"Young lady, please acknowledge his helpfulness, but don't make it mandatory to keep count. Learn to accept

gratitude graciously. That's one of the most ladylike gestures you can ever make," Mary admonished.

Later that morning, T.J. spoke, "Mr. Snowden, thank you for saddling my horse this morning. I'm sorry I caused you extra work. I didn't get much sleep last night, but I won't oversleep again."

"I know. You've done a good job this whole drive and in the delivery of that calf. I never thought you and your aunt could hold up your end so well, but could you do me a favor?"

"What's that?"

"Could you drop the Mr. Snowden, makes me feel like an old man? Call me Jed, like all the other hands do."

"Sure, if you'd call me T.J."

"That will be easy. Thanks again, T.J. Now I better get up front and see what's holding us up." Jed rode off to the west.

"He wasn't stand-offish, Mary."

"No, he's trying very hard to be decent to you. Let him, he's a decent man, so it comes naturally to him, whether you're a pretty young woman or the roughest old Shaker."

"Leave the *pretty* out of it, will you? I'm just one of the hands to him," T.J. said.

"I don't believe it for a minute," Mary replied.

"You'd better, because this is strictly a business arrangement."

"Sure! Did he saddle the other hands' horses this morning?"

"Mary, don't torment me. You know I'm right. He's never given a single word or gesture of anything else to me."

"He's an honorable man and beholden to you. He probably won't make a gesture, unless you give him leave to, or show him one first. His pride has to enter into it a bit. You know that male ego, we spoke of?" Mary reminded the younger woman.

"Never will I make the first gesture toward anything other than a business arrangement," T.J. spoke decisively.

"I wouldn't be totally sure of that missy, I think I've heard you say something like that before." Mary laughed at T.J.'s disgruntled expression and negative grunt.

The cows and calves were resting at the nooning when T.J. whirled around to look at the horizons. She spoke softly, "Isn't it beautiful?"

Jed looked at her face, while she gazed off at the sea of grass. He asked gently, "What's beautiful?"

"The greening of the prairie. It looks like green and gold water."

He looked away from her. "That's why they call it a sea of grass. See how it ripples." He looked toward the hills to the west, "Look way over there, how far do you suppose that is?"

"I don't know, Daddy always said it was further than it looks. Maybe five miles?"

"No, it's more like twenty," he said.

"How do you know that?"

"I've ridden to those foothills. It took me most of one day."

"With these calves it's going to take even longer," T.J. added.

"Yes, we can plan on almost two more days to reach those hills. We've got at least two more weeks before we get home at the rate we're going," Jed said.

"I'm nervous about what might happen to some of the calves, but isn't it wonderful out here? Smell the air. Look up at that hawk," T.J. pointed.

Jed watched T.J.'s face. "Beautiful. Yes, it is beautiful. Do you like it here?"

"How can you ask? Why wouldn't anyone love it here? It's open- spacious. I can't even describe it." She turned to look into his face, "Do you like it?"

"I wouldn't want to be anywhere else."

A calf bawled. A cow's answer brought them back to their task.

That evening after the ladies fixed supper, Jed walked away. He stood with his back toward the fire, looked at the starry sky.

"Mind if I join you?" T.J. asked.

Jed started and then apologized, "I just needed a little time alone."

"Oh, I'm sorry, I didn't mean to disturb you." T.J.

turned back toward the fire. *Why am I disappointed?*

"Come back, I've had my time. I didn't mean to send you away," he said.

"If you're sure?"

"I'm sure. Walk out a ways with me-   I'll show you the night."

"Should I tell Mary where I'm going?"

"We won't be long. She knows you can take care of yourself." His mind continued, *And if need be, I'll take care of you.*

"See those stars up there?" T.J. pointed. "Daddy used to say that was a dog star. It never looked much like a dog to me."

"Here, I'll show you," Jed pointed.

"I still can't see it," she said.

"Follow my finger."

T.J. stepped closer to let her eyes follow the line of Jed's arm and index finger against the clear night sky.

"There, see, my finger starts at the top, then comes down to the left," Jed's finger wavered when his attention shifted to T.J.

She turned to inquire as to his sudden silence. Discovering their closeness, she caught her breath, then stepped back. "I-   had better get back or I'll have problems getting up in the morning like I did after that calf was born."

He spoke quietly, "Think I'll stay out here for awhile. Good night, T.J."

She turned and walked quickly away toward the fire. Jed watched her shadow safely into the firelight. *I know I'll have a restless night if I go in now.* He walked further and further out into the grass of the prairie. Coyotes howled some distance away. *Lonely, that's a lonesome sound. Never thought about it before.*

Back at the campfire, T.J. and Mary quieted in their blankets. After a half hour, Mary heard T.J. sigh.

"What's the matter?" Mary asked.

"I don't know, just can't seem to get to sleep," T.J. said.

"Is it Jed?"

"I don't know, I just feel kind of lost tonight."

Mary chuckled, "Told you so."

"What's that supposed to mean?" T.J. asked.

"Can't figure it out for yourself? I told you one of these days you'd have an *all consuming interest* arise in your life. Think about it," Mary said.

T.J. sat up, punched her saddle blanket with her fist.

"Can't get comfortable?" Mary teased.

"No, I've got something scratchy under my blanket and it's keeping me awake."

"I think that's not all that's keeping you awake. Good night, girl."

T.J. stayed awake to hear Jed's steps when he came much later to his bedroll across the fire. She stayed very quiet, not wanting Jed to know she was still awake and bothered by her worry over him.

Jed settled down and worked his blanket up around his neck. *Lord, this is going to be a long two weeks. Help me know what is best for everyone.*

Soon, T.J. heard even breathing from across the fire.

I never knew men went to sleep so quickly or made such noises when they sleep. Guess I've heard more of their sleeping in the past month than I ever noticed before. When I was with my father out on the range, maybe I was too young and went to sleep first. We slept a little apart, maybe it was too far to hear them snore, or mutter in their sleep. Never noticed the night sounds so much either. Nice, all of it is very nice, comforting. Thank you Lord, I'm so drowsy. She drifted off to sleep.

Pleasant trailing days followed. The weather became milder as spring advanced, the grass grew; and the already born calves strengthened and new ones arrived. After eight days, they came upon Max with fifteen more cows and sixteen calves. The bossy old black cow had black baby bull twins.

"Maybe that was why she was so irritable," Jed commented.

"They're delightful, they look so alike, but they aren't quite as big as the others," T.J. noted.

"Sharing their maw makes for a little less milk. They're hardy though, they'll come along. Before you know it they'll be grazing and taking care of themselves," Jed said.

"I never saw so many calves of the same size together at once without extra mature cattle around," Mary commented.

"They are so much fun to watch. The old cows seem more peaceful," T.J. added.

"We're building up our herd fast," Jed turned toward the homestead. "Wonder how many more will be there when we get to home range?"

"Are you getting anxious to get home?" gently T.J. questioned.

"How'd you guess?" Jed confessed.

"It isn't too hard, but I hate to see this time end. I don't think I've ever had such a peaceful time in my whole life. Even though we've had some unusual things happen with the calving, it's been such a delightful time," she said.

Jed gave T.J. a happy and open smile.

She grinned in return.

His eyes changed. He looked away first, his smile gone as quickly as it had come.

T.J. turned away in confusion.

Jed thought he caught a look of misunderstanding and disappointment. He felt a pang of regret, as he watched her go. *I don't have anything to offer her, I'm going to pay her off as quick as I can. I can't keep her here any longer than necessary.*

Somehow the balance of their return to the home range carried an atmosphere of gloom, with only occasional blooms of spring breaking through their melancholy.

Jed didn't sleep well the nights T.J. stood watch. *Might as well be out there myself, I'd get as much rest.*

T.J. found herself awake when Jed stood watch too. One night she heard him get up and walk toward the rise. After an hour she walked out to keep him company.

Jed sat watching the stars, she could see his profile against the clear sky, his rifle standing at his shoulder. She spoke softly so as not to startle him, but he turned with his rifle half lowered.

"It's me, don't think I'm a coyote coming," she whispered.

She couldn't see his pleased expression.

"What's the matter, not getting enough work to tire you?" he asked.

"Guess not, I woke up and thought about keeping watch. I know it gets a little- quiet out here at night."

"Did you think you'd find me asleep on the job?" Jed asked.

"No, but four hours at night is a long time."

"Sometimes."

After a half hour of the two sitting quietly, Jed fidgeted, then spoke, "You'd better go in T.J., it will be getting light before you know it. We're getting near home and it's going to be a long day tomorrow."

"I 'spose."

She said no more, but rose and started back toward her rolled blankets.

Again, Jed thought she seemed a bit disappointed. I didn't purposely send her away, she needs her rest.

Who am I trying to fool?

Home Pastures

Finally, the cows and their young, rolled into home pastures in the southeastern corner of Colorado. The animals spread out over the greening pastures of the open prairie and grazed on the gentle hills and valleys.

"All set, think they're in good shape," Jed commented.

"Yes, now we can go back to the ranch house, get ourselves rested and back into our normal lives," Mary said.

"Don't they look wonderful in all this grass?" T.J. observed.

Jed looked at her, but made no comment.

In the next few days, Mary and T.J. adjusted to the return of household routine and the men back to the range and their work.

Mary took three fresh eggs from her apron pocket.

"I think the hens have settled in. T.J. look what they gave us."

"Eggs, let's eat them right now," T.J. laughed.

"Guess we can. We'll surely be getting more along," Mary added.

T.J. held up one of the eggs to the light as she might

a precious jewel.

"I'm sure glad Shaker got a dozen hens and a rooster at that farmstead in Kansas. I could just hug him for getting these for us," she gently lay the brown egg back in the pie plate.

"We'll have to save most of the eggs now that the hens have settled in, we can try to hatch some chicks," Mary said. "We'll put the hatching eggs in the cellar under the house and keep them cool until one of the hens starts setting. We'll need about ten eggs ahead and ready. I think that speckled hen is already a little broody so it may not be long before we can set her. We'll have to wait a few days to see if she'll set tight before we give her our precious eggs."

T.J. eyed the eggs on the table. "Guess I'd better put these in the cellar and wait a little later for my first taste of our very own eggs."

Mary noticed a missing enthusiasm in T.J.'s coming and going about their tasks.

"Are you unhappy?" she asked.

"No, not entirely. What's the matter with me? We've got plenty of work to do, food, a comfortable home. I had such a good time on the trail drive for awhile, then something happened. The last part wasn't as much fun. It seemed like we lost something coming back about a week out on the prairie."

Her aunt patted T.J.'s arm, "I'm not quite sure, but be patient. I think things will work out, given a little more time."

"Did I do something wrong?" T.J. asked.

"You always accuse me of complicating things, but I think you and Jed got a little too close and you both got scared," Mary commented.

"I do miss him. We saw so much of each other for a

few days and our- *friendship* was so easy. I really got to like him, he quit being so serious and bossy. He was real fun."

"If it's supposed to be, that will return. Why don't you go to the Lord, ask for patience and what's best for everyone?" her aunt advised.

"*Patience*, I never wanted patience in my whole life!" T.J. stormed.

"I know honey, that's why you might ask for it," Mary advised.

T.J. stomped up the stairs to her room. She threw herself on the bed and thumped her pillow. After fifteen minutes, she came back down the stairs.

"Mary, I'm going for a ride. Want to come along?"

"Can't right now, I've got bread just ready to punch down. You go on, but take your pistol along."

T.J. rode out. Over the next hour, she recaptured some of her awe from the trail. *Beautiful, no one can say it isn't beautiful, even though it's kind of- stark around here.*

The sun started to set. T.J. turned back toward the ranch house.

After that trip, she rode out every day, sometimes with Mary, sometimes alone.

Jed observed her coming and going, but he made a point of not coming too close to either of the two women.

With summer work, the men stayed away from their ranch quarters for days at a time. Even Shaker went along to feed the hands.

T.J. absently wandered toward the chicken coop early the next morning. The cool of the night was leaving. The rising sun gained strength. Inside the chicken coop was shaded and cool.

She reached under the red hen to check for eggs. The hen groused and pecked at her hand. The young woman persisted and shoved her hand under the hen's breast, she felt a cool surface and closed her hand. The egg moved.

T.J. jerked her hand from under the hen and lifted the old biddy to look among the feathers. A short diamond head raised and a forked tongue pattered in and out.

"Yipe," T.J. jerked her hand away and dropped the hen.

The hen settled back into the nest and ruffled her feathers with a growling sound.

T.J. backed from the building and screamed for her aunt.

"Mary, bring the hoe!"

Mary looked up. When she saw T.J.'s face, she picked up the hoe from where it leaned against the garden fence post. They both used the hoe for varmint threats.

"What is it?"

"There's a snake under the red hen. She isn't afraid of it, but I don't like it," T.J. shuddered.

"Here, use the leg hook and see if you can lift her off by the neck. I'll be ready and try to get it as soon as you have her out of the way," Mary directed.

T.J. slowly guided the chicken hook behind the hen's neck. "I may choke her or she may get bitten, but guess we don't have much choice. I sure don't want to come in here every day and have to gather eggs among the snakes. Are you ready?"

"I'm ready, jerk her straight up," Mary said.

T.J. lifted the hen straight up. The startled snake

reflexively struck to its full length.

The hen flopped loose and squawked off between T.J.'s legs.

"Get him while he's stretched out," she yelled.

Mary struck and struck. The snake threshed violently. He coiled around the hoe and Mary held the heavy short body down.

"Get the axe, I've got him, but I won't be able to move the hoe or he might get away."

T.J. rushed to the woodpile, twisted the axe from the block of wood and rushed to Mary's side.

"Hold him tight with the hoe and I'll be able to cut his head off clean." She came down with a short chop.

The body threshed more violently but the head snapped beside the axe blade.

Mary touched T.J.'s arm, "Step back and I'll let up on the hoe. Don't get on the head, it's as full of poison now as when it was attached."

T.J. retreated to the door and Mary gradually raised the hoe.

The two ladies stepped back and took a deep breath.

"Ma-a-ry, that could have been very dangerous," T.J.'s voice trembled.

"Yes, but we took care of it. Let's get out of here and go to the house. I need to sit down for a minute."

T.J. and Mary weaved to the house with their arms around each other.

"I'll never put my hand under a hen again without looking first," T.J. whispered.

"Good idea," Mary replied.

After a few minutes, Mary spoke again.

"I think we'd better move that snake and its head, then the speckled setting hen tonight when it gets dark. If anything hatches, there may be more critters on the prowl for the little ones. After all this work, I sure don't want to be producing food for all the snakes in the neighborhood."

"They probably smelled all that warm-blooded food and crawled under that hen after she sat down. Ugh, it still gives me the creeps just thinking about touching that coil and thinking it was a nice smooth egg." T.J. shuttered. "The cowboys kept warning us about prairie rattlers in our bedrolls or boots, but that's the closest I ever came to one and I never want to be that close again," she said.

"I heard a few buzzing when we were on the trail but the horses were as leery of them as I was and we walked around all of them," Mary added. "Did you know that some hog farmers turn their hogs into patches where rattle snakes might be? They claim the hogs will kill and eat the snakes."

"Let's get some hogs real quick," T.J. said. "We'll pen them all around the hen house and let them clean up the rattlers."

Mary laughed, "Sometimes hogs eat chickens too. We'd have to be sure all the chickens stayed out of the hog pen."

"You win some and you lose some, but I'd rather risk the hog than the snake," T.J. said. "Let's see if Jed or Shaker wants a hog the next time we do any traveling."

"I'm all for it," Mary nodded.

The Stray

Early one summer morning, Mary said to T.J., "Let's go to town and get some calico for new dresses and curtains. We need to liven this place up a bit."

"Good thought, I'd like that. It's getting a little too quiet around here with everyone else gone."

"Get your things and put your skirt in a bag on the saddle horn. We can ride with our trousers on and then put on a skirt when we get near town. Don't want to shock the good citizens," Mary added.

"Yes, let's make it a picnic of a day," T.J. added.

"Better leave a note, don't want to give someone a heart attack if they can't find us," Mary said.

The two rode away without looking back. They didn't see a rider approach the house and then go inside. Jed read the note on the table.

Think I'll go to town too. Make a nice outing for the day and the boys won't be back until tomorrow. Those women need an escort.

He washed, put on his clean shirt, slicked back his hair and ran to retrieve his ground-tied buckskin at the back door.

He rode to catch the women. As he crossed the trail behind them, he heard a mournful sound. He turned aside to investigate and found one of the calves bogged in the creek bed. Coyotes fled as he approached. On the bank, evidence of their hours on the scene and the cow's fighting them off showed.

By the time he had the little animal lassoed and out, it's mother had returned. He released the calf to her care and started on his way.

He had to ride harder than he had planned to catch the two before they reached town. He rounded the next to last turn and saw their horses ground-tied near a bush.

What's the matter now? He raised in his stirrups to look and caught a glimpse of white petticoat. *Whoops, they're changing clothes, better keep my distance.* He rode in a huge circle, came out on the trail between the women and town, sat and waited for the pair.

After fifteen minutes, he started ambling toward town. *I hear them coming, they'll soon catch up with me. I'll try not to embarrass any of us.*

"Hello, what are you doing on the way to town?" Mary was the first to speak.

T.J. hung back, looked away from Jed.

"I read your note, then cut across when I figured I was ahead of you, I slowed down. You've taken awhile to catch up to me. I was beginning to get worried about you two."

"We're fine, just had to change, so we wouldn't spook the townsfolk. Don't expect they're used to women in trousers," Mary commented.

"How are you T.J.?" he asked.

"I'm fine. Haven't seen much of you lately," she stated coldly.

"No, summer is a busy time on a ranch. We hayed down below the river, got that all up last week. This week, we've been working on this side. Thought I'd run into town for a few supplies, was going to ask you two to come along. When I got to the house, found your note and decided I'd catch up to you."

"How did you get here so fast?" T.J. asked. "I didn't know there was another trail."

"There isn't a good trail, but I can show you a short cut when we go back. That is, if we get started before it gets too dark. It's not a good place to be after dark, because there's some steep drop-offs and a person wouldn't want to make a misstep."

"Good. Let's hurry on to town and see what they've got in the general store." T.J. sat very straight in her saddle, one knee over the horn and her skirts settled on one side. She wasn't riding a side saddle, but few could have guessed.

Mary rode sedately on the other side of T.J.

I can't believe these are the two ladies who rode the trail with us. Big difference in appearances. Very handsome women. Hope I don't have to fight off a bunch of cowboys in town. Jed sat straighter in his saddle too. I'm proud to be seen with T.J., Mary too.

When they arrived in town they stopped before the general store.

Jed gave each of the ladies a hand down. He tied the three horses to the hitching rail in front of the store.

"I'll give my list to Mr. Cook and you ladies can go about your shopping. I'll meet you here in about two hours, if that's fine with you two. If we don't leave by then, it'll be too dark to take the cut-off to the ranch."

"We'll be here," T.J. turned on her heel to inspect goods on the other side of the store.

Mary slipped up behind T.J., "Kind of cool weren't you to Jed?"

"What would you expect? We haven't seen them for weeks and he wasn't too friendly the last few times he came around. If he wants us to be strangers, that's fine with me," T.J. turned away from Mary.

The ladies went about their business of shopping for the goods for dresses and curtains. They purchased a few sundry items and placed their purchases in their saddle bags.

"Let's walk around town. It seems months since we've been here. I've forgotten what town goings-on are all about," T.J. suggested.

"Look, those boys are tormenting some kind of little animal. Oh, mercy, how can they do such a thing?"

T.J. ran toward the small gang of boys gathered in a circle around some bedraggled little critter.

"Stop that! What kind of boys are you to be so mean to such a little helpless thing?" T.J. so startled the boys, they stepped aside. Several broke and ran when she continued her advance.

She scooped up the little animal before she could even see what it was. The dirty little fuzz ball cringed in her arms, afraid to raise its head. Blood dripped from a wound in its leg. T.J. looked around. No one came to claim the pup.

"Do you know who owns this puppy?" she asked the only boy brave enough to stand his ground.

"I don't think nobody does. It's been hangin' around for the past few days. It ain't very old, but no one wanted it in all that time." The boy ran off toward his wide-eyed friends.

T.J. turned and carried the pup back to Mary.

The clerk looked up, frowned and spoke, "Miss, can you please take that dirty little animal out of this store? The owner will have my hide if he catches it in here. He's already put it out several times."

"Can I have this pup?" she asked.

"That's fine by me. I don't think anyone will miss it."

"T.J., I think you'd better clear that with Jed. I don't think he'll mind, but it is *his* ranch," Mary commented.

"I'll keep it out of his way. I hope he won't object, because then I'd have to fight with him over it. I am going to take this pup home with us. If we can't keep him, at least we'll find a better place than this for him."

"All right, just go easy on your approach. Don't make demands until you've asked peaceably," Mary advised.

When Jed came into view, he was surprised to see the ladies huddled around the horses with their arms loaded. *I thought I'd have to go looking for them and they would continue to shop until dark.*

"You ladies finished before I did. Sorry I didn't get back sooner."

He looked first at Mary. She had a serious expression on her face. T.J. turned toward him with a stubborn stance. He looked down from her face. *What have I done now?*

What a dirty muff, didn't know she had one with her. The muff moved.

Jed sought to defuse the stormy look he saw, "Well, what have we here? Looks like that calf I pulled out of the mud on the way here."

"Some boys were tormenting this puppy. I picked it up and checked all around. The store clerk said no one belonged to the pup and they'd like to be rid of it. I told him we'd take it," T.J. deflated. She looked down at the matted bundle in her arms.

Jed softened. *I think I see a tear trying to creep from beneath her lashes. The tough lady going soft. Can't say I blame her, that little dog is pitiful. Hope he even lives, but I wouldn't bet on it.*

"We can take him home, but don't get your hopes too high. He don't look too healthy at the moment," he commented.

"Do you think we need to get something special for him to eat?" Mary asked. "He looks kind of young."

"I expect you ladies can make him some gruel or meat soup. I think that will work fine for his food, but he's got a ways to go. He's dripped blood on your dress. Here, let me hold him. Mary, why don't you go buy some toweling to wrap him in?"

"Thank you. I couldn't stand to see him suffer any longer," T.J. said.

"I know. I wouldn't want that either." Jed cleared his throat, he searched his memory for something to lighten the mood, but found nothing that seemed suitable. "When Mary comes back, wrap him up. I'll go load our supplies, then we'll be on our way."

The subdued trio rode from town together. They drew looks from idle men who stood about in front of the saloons and stores.

I'm glad to be leaving town, never thought about it being a problem for women before. These two used to walk out together by themselves before they got mixed up with us at the ranch. Jed prodded his horse to a faster gait, the ladies kept pace.

They remained quiet until the trail forked, one going toward the ranch, the other fainter trail leading off to the right and up over the hills.

"This is where we'd turn, if we were taking the short cut to the ranch, but tonight, I think we'd better get on home and take care of T.J.'s little orphan. That all right with you ladies?" Jed asked.

Mary thanked Jed.

T.J. nodded gratefully.

Longest trip I've ever made back from town, Jed brooded.

At Home

"Mary, do you think he needs food worse, or to be cleaned up?" T.J. asked.

"I think I'd give him food and let him rest first. He's not wet, so staying dirty won't hurt him another few hours."

"That was my thought too."

"When he's slept a while, we'll put on the boiler full of water. When it's warm, then we can clean him up," Mary added.

"I'm anxious to see what he looks like under all this dirt," T.J. said.

True to their word, the pup was fed, then collapsed with his head through a hole in an old blanket. He awakened much perkier. They put the warm water into an old dish pan. They used the lye soap and scrubbed him, then rinsed until no more dirt appeared in his water. T.J. toweled the little fellow dry.

He looked half his size with his puppy fuzz plastered down by the water. Rough bones poked through his wet hair.

Jed carried supplies into the kitchen. He rubbed the pup's ear between his fingers.

"Not much dog there. Thought he was bigger than that," he commented.

T.J. was defensive, "He'll grow."

"He's very thin and has been mistreated," Mary stated.

"Poor little fellow, wonder he's still alive," Jed scratched at the other ear.

"We've got to get him dried off before he takes cold. He can't stand too much in the condition he's in," T.J. got a fresh towel and rubbed him before the open oven.

"T.J., you're going to smother us all with the oven door open and that fire roaring like that." Jed turned the damper lower.

"I can't let him get chilled," she retorted.

"I know, I'm not bawling you out, just trying to make a bad situation lighter. I don't want you to be disappointed if he doesn't make it," Jed spoke gently.

"Remember, I was raised on a ranch. I've seen a few things die, had it happen to a few of my pets even. That's a part of life that I don't much like, but I'm kind of used to it."

T.J. raised the puppy up in the towel to look into his eyes. "Look, he's trying to lick my nose. I know he's going to get better. Just wait and see."

"If anyone can bring him around, I'm sure you can. Love goes a long ways toward healing many wounds. Your care is going to give that puppy *heart* and make him want to live," Jed said.

"Thanks, you make me feel a little better about his chances," she said.

"Well, I've got to get back to the men. We won't be back at ranch quarters for a few more days. You ladies take care of things, yourselves included." Jed walked out the door and swung up on the buckskin.

As an afterthought he turned, "If anything goes wrong, follow that dry creekbed there. You can't miss us in the hayfield on this side of the river."

"Thanks, we'll keep the home fires burning," Mary added a smile with her retort.

Jed smiled back, then saluted T.J. with a more sober face.

"I'll be seeing you both in a few days. You *three* rather." He looked at the pup, "Take good care of *our* pup."

Buddies

The pup lay on his side, he'd taken a turn for the worse. He hardly responded when the two women attempted to attend to him. T.J. and Mary rose several times each night to spoon more broth into the mouth of their little charge.

The liquid dribbled out on the cloth, little made its way down his throat.

The older woman rose at first light. She was aware that T.J. hardly came upstairs to bed during the night.

T.J. hung her head in despair. "Mary, are we doing him any favor? Would we be more merciful to put him out of his misery?" She sighed.

"Let me see how he looks this morning." Mary gently grasped the loose skin over the pup's neck. When she released it, the skin tented. "He's not getting enough liquids. We have to come up with some way to get more down him."

"I've tried to think of something all night, but anything I've used has just let more run out the other side of his mouth," T.J. lamented.

"If we tip his head up too much, we'll strangle him or give him pneumonia when we get fluid into his lungs," Mary added.

"Something hollow," T.J. looked around.

"I can't see anything in the kitchen. We could check the barn, but I'm doubtful."

T.J. jumped up. "A reed! There's some down on the river. I could ride down and cut some. Maybe we could pour some broth down him, if we could get it down his throat enough so he wouldn't choke."

Mary didn't think there was any hope, but it gave T.J. something to do and would take her mind off the immediate problem.

"Go ahead, I'll stay here and keep him warm. Be careful, don't want a drowned rat to take care of too." She attempted to lighten the mood.

T.J. threw on her trousers with a shirt. She left the house in a run. She was in such a hurry, she didn't saddle or spare her mare, but flew toward the river. The prairie dog town barked in alarm as she sped past.

She cast up and down the banks, then flung herself off at the first sight of reeds growing in the still backwater at the edge. She waded in, pulled out her knife and clipped a handful. She ran to where Bess stood, found a down tree trunk, and climbed aboard. She had the mare running before she settled firmly on her bare back.

"Boss, did you see that horse and rider go by about a mile away?" Shaker asked.

"No, who was it?"

"I would have sworn it was Miss T.J."

"She didn't come here to get us?" Jed asked.

"No, she was headed toward home."

"Maybe she couldn't find us. I'd better go check on

them," Jed moved toward the horses.

"Good idea, it seemed kind of strange."

Jed hollered back to Shaker as he grabbed his horse and threw on the saddle. "I'll be back as soon as I can. If we've got trouble, I'll get you word."

Oh God, please don't let those women be in real trouble. Jed raced his horse at full speed toward the ranch house.

When he rode into the yard, he threw down his reins, leaped up on the porch and through the back door.

Sitting on the floor were the two women intently involved with a wrapped bundle in their lap. A reed protruded from the mouth of the lifeless pup. Mary attempted to pour broth down the reed. They barely acknowledged his presence with a nod of their heads.

Jed stopped, planted his hands on his hips and observed for a few minutes.

"Are you two all right?" he asked.

They didn't reply.

He wanted more. "What in the world are you doing?"

Mary answered, "Which question do you want answered first?"

"Take your choice." He could see they were in no imminent danger.

"We decided this little fellow wasn't getting enough liquids, so we're trying to get something down him that won't dribble out the other side of his mouth," T.J. answered. "That should be obvious."

Jed squatted next to the threesome. "No, never saw anything quite like you're doing. I do assume you two ladies are fine? You forgot to answer that one."

"We're busy right now, can't get this in his lungs or we'll suffocate him," T.J. said.

Jed spoke gently. "You kind of scared Shaker. He was up on high ground and saw you running your mare. He was afraid someone was hurt or something, and maybe you couldn't find us," he answered stiffly.

"We're fine. Just doing our best to bring this pup around," Mary tossed over her shoulder as she dipped more broth with a spoon.

"Well, if you don't need my help, I'll be going?"

"I guess we're doing the best we can. He's not doing very well," T.J.'s voice caught.

Jed had the urge to comfort her, but stopped his hand half way to her back. He dropped his hand.

Mary observed his movement. When he raised his head, their eyes met above T.J.'s bowed one. A look of understanding passed between them.

"Be careful of the prairie dog holes if you go out again. There are some in that valley near the river. Sure can injure a horse and give you a spill." He pushed his hat back and continued, "We'll be back tomorrow. Hope things are going better by then." He turned slowly and went back outside. He reached for the reins on T.J.'s horse and led her toward the barn. After he put the bridle on the rack, he rubbed the mare down with a whisk of straw, then turned her out in the corral next to the barn.

He walked back toward his horse near the porch.

T.J. stuck her head out the door. "Thanks for coming back and putting my horse away. We'll try not to scare you again." She raised her gaze to look at him. "How are things going with the haying?"

"Fine, we're almost finished. The boys will ride back from the other side of the foothills by tonight, then we'll all be in tomorrow," he said.

"How about Mary and I fixing you all a hearty meal for tomorrow evening?" she asked.

"You sure your little charge can spare you ladies?" came Jed's soft question.

"Yes, one way or the other, we'll have time to fix a good meal."

Jed got the distinct impression she looked down to stop the revelation of her attachment to the pup. His heart twisted for her.

"Hope you have a better day. We'll be seeing you for supper tomorrow evening." He swung aboard his buckskin and rode slowly toward the river.

The next morning, T.J. came to the kitchen rubbing her eyes. Her appearance relayed another rough night. Her first movement was to look at the pup. She stroked him gently with one finger over the crown of his head, then continued to finger an ear.

"I think he's taking a turn for the better. He actually raised his head and wagged his tail about three this morning," T.J. said.

"Good, it seemed to me he was stronger at six. Look, his skin doesn't stick up so bad. I think he's resting a little easier too," Mary added.

"He doesn't seem to be breathing quite so hard," T.J. observed.

"If he continues to progress today, he just may come around," Mary said.

"Have you ever noticed how quickly young animals recover if they get proper care?" T.J. asked.

"Yes, God's creations are marvelously well thought out." Mary turned to look at T.J.

"Well, young lady, are you ready for your breakfast? I have a huge meal fixed and if we are feeding the men tonight, we'd better get to our bread and pie making before too much longer."

"Just let me sit here a minte and then I'll be able to get moving." T.J. rested her forehead on her hand.

Mary looked at the exhausted girl. "Do you want this coffee to wake yourself up?"

"Huh? Oh, what did you say? I think I dozed off again," T.J. answered.

"Do you want some coffee?"

"Sure." She toyed with a few bites of food.

"T.J., why don't you go back to bed for an hour or so? I'll get the bread going, then when you get up again, you'll feel more like yourself."

"Have you fed the pup?" the young woman asked.

"Yes, he's full and resting easy."

"Think I will for a few minutes." T.J. stumbled back up the stairs and collapsed onto her bed.

Three hours later, Mary awakened her when she placed the back of her hand on the young woman's forehead. "You're not sick too, are you?"

"No, what time is it?" T.J. scrambled up and pulled on her work clothes. "Why didn't you get me up sooner? I can tell by the sun in the window it must be nearly noon."

"That's fine, things are going along well on the meal and you needed your rest. Worry will take a lot out of a person, and you've been worried for several days about that pup. I think it's about time you came downstairs and took a peep at him."

T.J. turned a worried face, "Is he worse?"

Mary turned, "Come and see."

T.J. beat her aunt down the stairs and hurried to the wood box by the stove.

"Hi, fellow."

The pup squirmed. "Oh, Mary, he's trying to get up. He's a whole lot better!"

"Yes, not well, but better. We'll have a few more tough days, but we're getting there."

"Oh, I'm so relieved," T.J. breathed.

While Mary peeled potatoes for their supper, she overheard T.J. singing as she dusted the furniture in the house.

Celebration reigned that evening when the men filed into the big kitchen. The long trestle table was laden under the fruits of everyone's labor. A huge beef roast centered the table, surrounded by mashed potatoes, green beans, gravy, fruit jelly, fresh bread, butter, and cold drinks made a hearty meal, followed by slices of dried apple pie.

The men ate in contented silence.

Shaker pushed back his chair first and rubbed his stomach appreciatively. "Thought I was tired of beef, but that sure tasted good, Ma'ams. Thankee."

"Yes, Ma'ams," circled the table, as the men scraped back their chairs.

"I'm gonna go sleep for a week. Plumb tuckered out," Shaker said.

"We're glad you're back. Take it easy tomorrow," T.J. said.

Jed rose, "Yes, we've all worked hard. Everyone, I appreciate it. You take tomorrow off. We'll get back to it the day after that." He pushed his chair in and turned to go.

"Thank you ladies." He looked away and stepped to the porch. "Fine meal," he spoke back through the partially open door.

T.J. watched him walk out across the ranch yard. She put her hands on her hips, "What did I do that time?"

"Theodosia! I think you might have shamed him when you suggested the men take it easy. He *is* the boss, don't you remember? Don't you think he should tell the men what to do?"

"I meant for him to rest too. It was just a suggestion, not an order," T.J. huffed.

"You demean him in front of the men when you make suggestions. You might watch your tone of voice, sometimes your suggestions sound like orders."

"Oh," T.J. turned and went up the steps to her bedroom. In frustration, she settled herself on the edge of the bed and flopped to her back, her feet still on the floor. *Dear God, why can't I ever do anything right for that man?* She turned to her side and closed her eyes.

She must have drifted off to sleep, she found herself in another world. Jed was asking her for a dance at a fine ball, somewhere in a city. For once, she truly looked into his face and fluttered her lashes.

"Why yes, Sir, I'd be delighted." She felt herself rise and float out onto the floor with her hand in his.

She awoke with a start, "Hogwash, I never fluttered

my eyelashes in my whole life- but the dance was nice."
*Maybe you should act lady-like sometime and not be
so overbearing.*

"Who said that?" T.J. sat up and looked around.
Mary's not in the room. T.J. found no one else in the room.
God did you speak to me?

*How about your conscience? You might listen to it
once in a while, I put it there for a purpose.*

T.J. rolled to her knees beside her bed. "Lord, forgive
me. I know I am arrogant and-   spoiled. My daddy let me
have my way and now, it causes me problems all the time."
She stayed very quiet for several minutes.

*You are responsible and only YOU. You can not
blame your father for giving you what you wanted. Learn to
accept what you have and be kind to those around you. If you
don't, you will hurt others and life will be very long and
lonely for you.*

When T.J. came back down stairs, Mary noted a quiet
and pensive mood.

"T.J. are you all right, you seem quiet?" Mary asked.

"Yes. I have to admit, I've done a little soul-searching
and I wasn't too happy with what I saw. I'm sorry, Mary. I
know I'm not always the easiest person to live with. Will you
forgive me for taking you for granted? I promise I will try to
do better. I will work on some of my short comings too."

Mary hugged the girl to her. "Sure, I love you for who
you are. God made you unique, don't lose that specialness that
He gave you."

"Thank you, Mary. I love you too." She hugged her
aunt. "You're so good to me, I don't know what I'd do
without you."

"Me either. I think we all have a few traits to work on," Mary added.

The next day, T.J. surprised Mary with a comment. "I'm going to call him Buddy."

"What? What was that you said, T.J.?"

"I'm going to call the pup Buddy. He's my buddy."

"Do you think you should name him yet?" Mary asked quietly.

"Yes, because if I don't, that will be an admission he won't make it and I think he will now," T.J. said.

"I think you're right, but we still need to be cautious," Mary added.

"The next few weeks will be hard ones for him as he tries to get on some solid food. What can we feed him?"

"Why don't we scrape some of that left-over roast beef and add that to the beef gruel we've been feeding him?" Mary said.

"That ought to be more strengthening. Let's do that, right now," T.J. crowed.

After two more days, T.J. sat on the porch in the sun with the pup in his box.

"Sunshine and fresh air are good for what ails a body. Don't you think so, Buddy?"

"What did you say?" a masculine voice spoke as it came around the side of the house.

T.J.'s head jerked around. "Why do you always creep up on me?" Anger crept into her question.

"Do I?" Jed asked.

Remembering her new vows, she rethought her answer. "I'm sorry. I was thinking out loud and didn't know anyone was around."

"Sorry to interrupt your conversation, but we need a few things, would you and Mary mind going to town for us?" he asked.

"Sure. Come into the kitchen and make us a list. I'll get Mary and we'll be on our way."

"Aunt Mary, let's try the cut-off," T.J. rode ahead.

"Umh, I'm not sure we should without telling someone first. If we have problems no one will know where to look for us," Mary advised.

"Come on, we've got all afternoon. We can go slow, then we can come back by the old trail when we go home,"T.J. pleaded.

"All right, but ride carefully. Jed said there were some steep drop offs. We sure don't want to get into trouble out here."

Halfway through the trail the two edged along a steep ledge. At a bend T.J. stopped Bess.

Mary spoke, "Looks to me like there's been a slide. We'd better go back. I don't think the horses can make it without sliding. Then we wouldn't be able to get back on the trail."

How are we going to turn around on this narrow trail?" T.J. asked.

Mary looked around. "I don't think we can, it's not wide enough."

"We'll have to back up a few feet. Bess can do it."

Mary looked doubtful. "I'm not sure, but let's give it

a try."

"My horse won't back," she sounded in frustration.

"Maybe you can get off and back him from the ground," T.J. suggested.

"There's hardly room to get off," Mary said.

"You've got to do something. Bess can't move until your horse is out of the way," T.J. said.

"All right, here goes."

Mary eased out of the saddle and slid down her horse's side. She stayed as close to the animal as she could. She reached for the ground. Her foot slipped off the edge of the trail.

"I don't think there's room for me here!" Mary's voice was intense.

"I've got more room. I'll get off and help you. Bess will ground tie and stay put."

T.J. tossed Bess' reins down either side and dismounted close to her side.

She put her left hand against the rock wall and crept quietly toward Mary's horse. She took the reins below the bit.

"Mary, I'm afraid you may over balance him if you stay on the side."

Mary tried to pull up with her arms. "I can't reach the stirrup. He's too tall."

The saddle moved with her weight.

"Mary, take your left hand off and get a handful of his mane," T.J. directed.

The saddle moved more with Mary, but she managed to grab a handful of mane with her left hand.

"All right, I'll try to back him up. Keep a good grip on

his mane. If the saddle turns clear over it will push you further out over the slide and make it harder to hold on. Are you ready? I'll try to back him now."

T.J. pushed on the bit and leaned her shoulder into his chest. He side stepped and swung Mary further out over the slide.

"Careful, T.J."

"Let's try it again. Ready?"

She pushed again. "Back, back."

The horse took three steps back and became skittish.

Mary spoke softly, "Let him rest a moment. Then try again."

"Are you getting tired? Don't want you to let go," T.J. said.

Mary looked behind her horse.

"If you can get him ten feet further, there will be room for me to get off."

"Let's go again. Back, back," T.J. coaxed.

The horse moved three feet then fretted again. He threw his head back to relieve the pressure on the bit.

T.J. let up on the reins, she soothed with her voice and a pat on the nose.

He settled.

"Just a little further," Mary breathed.

T.J. spoke, "Back, back," without pressure on the bit. She pushed her shoulder on his chest. He eased back.

"Is that enough?" she asked.

Mary looked at the trail. "See if you can squeeze him against the wall."

T.J. took the left rein and pushed on the horse's

shoulder. He tossed his head and she staggered, but held to the rein.

"That was close. He almost knocked you off, " Mary breathed.

T.J. recovered her breath.

"Let's give it one more try. Be ready to step off if there's enough room," T.J. directed.

"All right, here goes."

Mary slid her hand down the saddle strings. She wrapped the longest around her hand and lowered herself to its full length. Her right toe touched the trail. She reached with her left hand and grasped the tow sack tied to the front strings.

"I'm down," Mary breathed.

"Step up here in front and we'll rest a minute," T.J. said.

The two sank to the rock wall.

Both horses dropped their heads, fully relaxed.

"Are you ready to try to force him further back down the trail?" T.J. asked.

"All right. You take the reins and I'll push on his shoulder."

"Back, back. He's going!"

The horse stepped a hind foot off the trail. He started and took two steps forward.

"Whoa, steady," T.J. soothed.

"Let's try again. We can soon turn him around," Mary said.

"All right, I'll take the reins and see if he'll turn. I'll go past him so he can't knock me off," T.J. volunteered.

She turned the horse's head to the rear. He bent in the middle an brought his front feet around. Halfway, he panicked when a foot slipped over the edge. He jerked the reins from T.J.'s hands and turned back facing the slide.

"We'll have to back him further, he's too afraid to turn," Mary said. "Come back in front of him."

T.J. patted the horse's hip and slipped beside him.

"I probably could get on. He might back better if the reins were being pulled from the rear."

"I don't think you should be on him, he's too spooked," Mary said.

"We could tie the rope to the reins and back him from the ground behind him. Let's give it a try."

T.J. reached over the horse's withers to knot the lasso to the right rein. Then to the left on her side. She moved beside and to the rear of the horse again.

The lasso dropped to the horse's middle. He shifted nervously when it touched his haunch.

"I think I'd better try to thread the lasso through the rear saddle strings so it won't get into his flanks. He's better if we keep everything high up on his back.

She dropped the rope on the trail.

"Whoa," she placed her hand on his hip and moved close beside him again. She looped the strings around the lasso and moved back to pick up the rope.

"Here goes. Push on his shoulder and we'll give it another try."

"Back, back." Both women spoke to the horse. He moved three, four and then five steps back. He bowed his body to the wall. T.J. dropped the left lasso and pulled on the right end.

He bent and turned around.

T.J. threw her arms around the gelding's neck and buried her face. Tears stung her eyes.

Mary looked back at her. "We got him."

"Let me catch my breath." Mary placed her hand on her knees and bent from the waist. She regained her composure and asked, "Do you want to me to bring Bess?" Mary asked.

"All right. Pick up the reins and speak to her. I think she'll back, just keep her straight and don't back off the trail.".

Mary slipped by Bess' side and grasped the reins below the bit.

She spoke to Bess, "Back, back."

The mare stepped back calmly.

"Whoa!" T.J. called. "Move her up a step and into the wall, she's gotten too far out."

Mary did as T.J. instructed. She moved Bess forward, then back the ten feet she needed. Mary moved by Bess and the horse turned sharply with her.

"Thank God, we got that done," Mary breathed.

T.J. said, "I never plan to use this short cut again. That's what I get for being impetuous. I'll think twice next time. Drop Bess' reins and come on up here. I'll hold him until you get aboard."

Mary did as directed.

As soon as she was aboard, she allowed the horse to move forward into a wider section of the trail.

"I'll never take out a horse on the trail again we haven't trained to back first," T.J. said.

When they were underway, T.J. spit on her hands.

"Are you hurt?" Mary asked.

"He burned my hands when he jerked the reins away. They'll be fine when I get a little salve on them."

That night, both thanked their God for safety on their trip.

Mary started to tremble when she recalled all that might have happened.

Thank you, God. Help me to have peace over our experience. She calmed and drifted off to sleep to be awakened in the night by a cry.

What was that? It's coming from T.J.'s room.

She entered the hallway and knocked lightly, "T.J. are you all right?"

She received no answer; pushed open the door to find T.J. uncovered and damp with perspiration. Mary felt of her forehead.

T.J. startled awake.

"I was having a nightmare," she said.

"What were you dreaming?" Mary asked softly.

"About that short cut."

Mary clasped T.J. in her arms. She rocked the younger woman and stroked her back.

"Sh, sh, it's all right baby." She poured water into the basin and wrung out a cloth. She wiped T.J.'s face and arms, then handed the girl a towel.

"Thank you, Aunt Mary."

"Do you want me to stay with you?" Mary asked.

"Would you?"

"Sure, you're still my little girl." Mary stretched out at T.J.'s back and continued a soothing back rub. She picked up a lullaby and began to hum.

T.J. gradually relaxed and Mary's humming stopped.

Both slept till sunrise.

Another Problem

To add to his problems, Jed found a calf with a broken front leg stuck in a den at the prairie dog town. He and the hands tied her down on to the sled and moved her to the ranch house where they slung her upright to the rafters in the barn. They splinted the broken leg with small boards and an old sheet they tore into strips.

T.J. and Mary fed and watered this new charge when they milked each day.

The ladies began to call the heifer, Crip, for want of a better designation.

In several months, the calf's leg strengthened and the men lowered her to support part of her own weight on the mending leg.

"Her leg is a little crooked but I think she'll be able to walk soon. We'll soon put her out with the milk cows to finish recuperating. Can't lose any of our stock if we can keep from it," Jed said to Shaker.

"The women have gotten partial to her. They can't seem to keep from makin' pets of the stock around the house," Shaker added.

"Guess it's just their nature. My mother was that way too," Jed said. "Well, we better get back to work. It'll be time to get more water by tomorrow."

Round Up

With Crip in the home pasture with the milk cows and their calves, the ladies were free to go out with the supply wagon.

Mary cooked or helped Shaker, while T.J. helped corral the stock to be worked.

The seasons advanced, the calves were worked and branded, hay was hauled to ricks that circled the ranch house. Jed never intended for his cattle, or hands to be far from his house to be caught in another blizzard. His own experience had imprinted the grave danger upon his mind. He planned and worked accordingly.

The abundant grass fed the scarce number of cows. His cattle and their offspring made huge progress in the short summer months. Fall approached and with the first snows, the animals were gathered into corrals near headquarters.

When they tallied the cows, there were four hundred and ninety three with four hundred and forty calves. They had gained some abandoned and unbranded adult stock from the range. They had lost some calves since birth, however.

"We're set for winter here. We keep seeing those mustangs off toward the hills, now that we're caught up, we'll go out and try to catch a few," Jed directed his hands.

They built a corral against the hillside and around the

water hole. The crew backed off for a few days and allowed the horses to come undisturbed to water.

After a week, Shaker and Jed lay in wait on the hill above the spring.

Shaker whispered near Jed's elbow. "That one mare don't look like them others, and that colt must a been on his way before she joined up with this bunch."

"He's a dandy. She looks like a Morgan to me with that proud carriage. I haven't seen that quality around here before. She must have gotten loose from someone traveling through, because she's not branded," Jed said. "He might be out of an eastern horse or one of those army studs they turned loose after catching some of the wild stallions. If we can catch those two, I'd be mighty pleased. Tomorrow, let's bring out the hands and be set and try for the gate."

The next morning before daylight, Jed placed his men and the ladies.

"I'll come in from the gate side, you all swoop in behind me and circle the pen. Go to any spot where they seem to want to crowd out. Keep them away from the fence until they settle down, then we can catch them and snub the wild ones to our stock. We'll take them back to the ranch and see what we can do with them."

The men and T.J. were on their horses and ready when Jed crept down a draw to the corral gate.

An old mare threw up her head and snorted. The herd bunched and looked toward the direction she stared.

She wheeled and dashed toward the gate. Jed got there right after she exited and hit for the hills. The band attempted to follow but he waved his duster and managed to pull the bars closed in the gate.

The harem leader ran some mares over the fence on

one side. They escaped before the hands could close the gap

The remaining younger stock milled in the center of the corral, securely penned..

Plans came about as they had hoped. When the dust settled, there were three mares and four colts left in the pen.

Jed looked over the captives. "We got that colt we wanted, but not his mother. Fix the fence and let them settle a bit."

The men tied their horses to available scrub around the pen and scrambled to reinforce the weak spots.

The captured animals milled and called.

"The herd boss is over there on the hill. Do you want to try for him?" Max asked.

"No, we got about all we can handle here and if we can get them caught and back to the ranch without injury, this will be enough. I sure would like to get that one mare though. Maybe we can figure something out once we get these secured. Let's see if we can catch them," Jed directed.

The men opened the gate and circled quietly on their horses.

The crew on the outside watched for attempts to break out.

Shaker caught the first colt with his lasso. Max caught another and Casey caught one of the mares. They anchored the animals to gentle ranch horses and went back for the rest.

One by one the wild animals were subdued.

"You fellows take those back to the ranch. I think I'll stake out this colt and see if I can entice his mother back for him," Jed said. "Leave us an extra horse and we'll be in as soon as we can."

T.J. looked around. *I mean to stay.*

"Let's use Bess for the holding mare. She's gentle and won't hurt the little guy," she suggested.

"Good idea, she's about the most gentle of all the horses in our bunch," Jed agreed. "Tie her to the center post so that herd boss won't come back and run her off. We've got to leave the gate open."

"Won't he hurt her?" T.J. asked.

" We'll be close by and ready, so he won't have time to hurt her," Jed assured.

They yoked the frantic horse colt to Bess and opened the gate. She indulgently tolerated his bucking and kicking. In a short time, the little horse hunkered by her side and settled for a fretful night.

Jed rode up and behind a swag in the hill. T.J. followed on the ranch horse.

"We'll settle down here on watch during the night and keep quiet. Leave your horse saddled and ready. If we don't get predators, by morning that little guy will be sounding off calling in his mom. I'd expect her to come back looking for him by daylight," Jed said.

After some hours, clouds obliterated the moon and it grew dark.

Jed reached for T.J.'s arm.

She tilted her head toward his ear, "I hear it. Something's coming."

"It rumbling, think it's the mare," Jed said.

"Could be the herd boss," T.J. speculated.

"Look at Bess and the colt, they're looking off to the west. The colt is answering," Jed said. "Get aboard and be ready to move when she gets in the corral."

Quietly the pair mounted up. They could see the

shadow of a horse moving cautiously through the gate of the pen. It stopped to smell the ground and listen often.

The animal approached Bess and rumbled. The colt thrashed and fought to loosen the yoke. Bess turned with the intruder. It circled and came at her with fierce defiance.

The three animals were distracted.

"Now, let's go," Jed whispered.

He slid down the hill and into the gap of the corral.

He bounded off and drew the poles across the opening.

T.J. followed close behind. She handed him more poles.

"Got 'em. Let's see what. Stay here by the gate in case they make a break for it." He mounted his horse and rode around the three in the center of the corral.

Jed circled. "It's the colt's mother. She doesn't act too wild. Let me see if I can snag her."

Jed flipped out his loop and let fly. The loop settled over the mare's head and she ceased moving.

"She's broke to a rope. Let me get her snubbed and we can untie Bess and the colt and start for home."

All secure, T.J. threw back the gate poles and lowered several sections of the fence.

Jed rode to Bess' head and untied her halter. "You take her lead rein and let her take this little fellow in. I'll keep this mare dallied to my saddle. Stay close enough to keep her moving. I think the colt will go fairly peacefully with his mother and Bess."

Jed led off. Bess and the colt followed close behind. The mare turned back often to assure herself her colt followed.

"Drive Bess up beside the mare, she's fretting about

her colt," Jed directed.

T.J. did as directed and the five struck out for home.

Minor altercations occurred between Bess and the colt but he was no match for the seasoned mare.

T.J. spoke to the colt, "You can nurse when we get home. You're old enough to wean, you surely can hang in there a bit longer."

The colt flicked intelligent ears toward the strange sounds of human voices.

In two hours, they reached the home corral and placed the colt and his mother in the high pen with the other recent acquisitions.

The colt shook his head and headed for his mother as soon as they loosened his tether.

The hands had filed out of the bunk house and Mary out of the house as soon as she heard the commotion. They all joined Jed and T.J. where they watched the new horses in the breaking pen.

Jed spoke to them all, "Good job. That's about all we can afford to feed this winter, but we made a good haul. This young stock will grow up before we know it. If that last colt grows out the way I expect, we'll have a good one for improvement of our own stock."

"Are you going to wean them soon?" T.J. asked.

"Yes, we'll give them some time to settle down, then we'll put an old gelding or Bess in with them and move the mares into another corral," Jed answered.

He turned to T.J., "In a couple of weeks, can you spare Bess for a few days?"

"That will be fine, she'd keep them from panicking and

doing something dangerous. We've got other horses I can ride. At home, we took away the nurse horse once in a while. They've got to learn to be without her sometime," T.J. said.

Jed turned to his crew, "Well, everyone get some rest today and we'll start on these adult horses tomorrow. They will need to be branded soon. They're probably all in foal, we won't need to handle them roughly after some initial work and branding," Jed instructed.

The men turned from the corral. Mary and T.J. stood to watch the colts settle and start to graze.

T.J. walked to the stock tank which extended into the breaking pen. She dipped her hands into the water and dampened her face.

Mary looked at her exhilarated niece, "Let's go inside, T.J., you need a nap. I'll fix you some bacon and eggs. We've got some biscuits left. You can settle in for a time. Did you enjoy watching for that mare?"

"We stayed alert and had the horses saddled all night. She came in about four and then we got busy shutting the gate and catching her. She seems to be broken to lead so she didn't give us any trouble once we had the noose around her neck. She may even be broke to saddle. Look at that little tuft of white hair behind her left front leg. It looks like a little saddle wear to me."

"Glad it was such an easy job. She is a good looking mare. She'll be an asset to the ranch," Mary said.

❄

Several severe winter storms hit again, almost a repeat of the year before, but this time Jed and his hands were prepared. The cows and horses were bedded down near the shelter of the ricks.

Pens around the ricks were opened every few days to allow the animals to forage on new ricks that sustained their lives. The winter proved difficult, but not impossible on the animals or the hands.

Many surrounding ranchers again lost their meager herds, but due to their advance planning, Jed's ranch lost few. Despite their good care, some weaker animals succumbed to the bitter weather.

The ranch folk were tired and grew irritable- too much winter and cold sapped their spirits.

T.J. hadn't seen Jed for days. He stayed at the bunkhouse and seemed to avoid the house.

As snow thawed from the latest blow, she spotted him walking around and round the outside corral with his head down.

She intercepted him on his third trip. She tried to engage him in conversation, but he barely answered.

"Jed, I can't help but know you must be worried. In town, they said most of the ranchers had lost their stock again."

"I am grateful we moved our stock in and didn't have any more. I had hoped we could find others, but now, I'm glad we didn't," Jed commented.

"Have we lost many?" she asked.

"Maybe fifteen head."

"Oh, I'm sorry." T.J. looked at Jed. "What else aren't you telling me?"

"Your heifer is still alive," he commented.

"I keep trying to tell you, she's not my heifer, she belongs to you."

Distracted, he shoved his hat back and rubbed the back of his neck. "Crip didn't make it."

T.J. paled, "We knew she was at risk after that broken

leg. I'm sorry but some animals aren't strong enough to make it, but that's part of ranching, no matter how much we hate that part of it."

"If this keeps up, everyone in this area will be out of business before long," Jed said.

"Don't forget, I still have some money drawing interest. This surely can't go on much longer. You can use my extra money," she stated.

"No! I can't do that, I'll have to tell you that with things the way they are, I may not even be able to pay you and Mary's allowances this year."

For once, T.J. kept her mouth shut for a moment. *Got to watch that ego, or I'll shame him again.* "Keep my extra funds in mind if we need feed or something else for the cattle."

She went back to the house, "Mary, we lost Crip to the weather. I don't think Jed wanted to tell me, but he probably knew we'd find out. I had to act like I didn't care too much because he's worried about the stock again."

"Good girl, I'm glad you were able to keep calm for Jed, he's had about all a rancher can take lately," Mary said.

"She was a sweet little heifer but guess it wasn't meant to be." T.J. wiped a single tear from her cheek.

They dragged through until spring and the cows could go back out on the lush pastures. The yearlings were put on other ranges to fatten. Prospects looked good for selling them in the fall.

Not Another Problem!

No further rains came, the grass drooped, then dried.

Mary opened the cap on the barn cistern to draw water for the milk cows. A piercing, repulsive odor met her nostrils. She covered her face with the sleeve of her dress and peered down. There in the bottom of the jug shaped rock-lined cavern paddled a bedraggled, wet animal with white stripes V'ed on its back.

"A skunk!" *How do I get him out without making it worse and getting his scent all over myself?*

She crouched to scoot the cap back on the well and backed up.

Shaker came from the bunk house. "Where's that smell comin' from?"

Mary looked at him. "I'm afraid it's coming from the barn well. I put the lid back on but I haven't figured out how to get it out yet."

"I know how. I'll be back shortly," he stated.

Shaker turned on his heel and walked into the barn where a set of handmade fishing poles hung in the rafters. He stepped up on the gate and drew down the heaviest pole. He removed the line, split the end of the stick and advanced on the well.

"Miss Mary, you best go into the house, this ain't gonna be pretty or smell good," he said.

"Are you sure you don't need help?" Mary asked.

"Ma'am, I can handle it." He angled his head toward the house and jerked his directions.

"Hate to leave you with this, but since you said so, I'm not waiting around for more of this smell." Mary scooted toward the house her eyes streaming tears from the acrid smell.

Shaker pulled the cap from the well, widened the split in the end, and lowered the pole. He pushed the skunk against the wall of the cistern and twisted the stick. The loose fur on the nape of the skunk's neck was caught in the split.

"Here goes kitty. Outta my way!" He drew the stick up and flipped the whole mess to his right. Shaker ran in the opposite direction.

When the skunk hit the ground, it twisted to bite at the object binding his neck. He came loose and turned his rear to use his most common defense, an offensive spray. His weapon was now depleted by his adventures in the well. When no one came near, he shook his fur and ambled away.

Mary and T.J. watched from the window of the ranch house and Shaker from the door of the barn.

No one wanted to go outside for the next few hours.

During the afternoon, T.J. and Mary observed Shaker hauling a number of barrels of water and dumping them into the cistern.

He scrubbed down the walls with a long handled brush, drew off the water and rinsed with more water.

He came to the back porch.

Mary answered his tentative knock T.J. stood behind her aunt.

"Ma'am, I think the well's fine now. I put some water in the trough for the cows. I laid a net over it to keep Buddy out. We'll leave the top off-   let it air out for a day or two, then I think we can use it again. I think that ole skunk just wanted a drink and he didn't bargain on it bein' so far down."

"Thank you, Shaker. I'm sure glad you knew how to get that skunk out. I would have shot him and that would have made things even worse," T.J. said.

Mary looked out the window. She watched Shaker walk away. He lifted his shirt sleeve to his nose and sniffed. In about an hour, she saw his shirt and jeans hanging on the clothesline.

"Do you think he got that smell out?" Mary asked.

"We'll know in a day or so, but with so much of it around here, it will be hard to tell. I can even smell it inside the house," T.J. remarked.

"That may be from me. I raised that lid and almost got overpowered . Maybe I'd better soak these clothes too," Mary went up the stairs to take care of her clothing too.

She soon returned with wet hair and her clothes wrapped in a towel. She put them outside on the back porch.

The drought continued.

T.J. and Mary hauled barrels of water from the artesian wells to the dried up house cistern for their household needs.

The men hauled barrels of water to keep the stock tank filled for the horses and the animals pastured near the ranch house.

A few wild strays gathered around the stock tanks and overturned the barrels to reach the precious water. These animals threatened any of the hands who were foolish enough to approach on foot.

Prairie fires dashed across the distant plains, bringing acrid smoke that burned the eyes and pinched the nostrils. Worried looks were exchanged as the hands rode out frequently, checking water holes and bogs for cattle seeking water and floundering until they were stuck fast. Each hand pulled several from the mud. Coyotes again feasted on the dead.

Trying to help, T.J. commenced riding a circuit too. Buddy loped along to occasionally chase a fleeing jackrabbit, until he tired and returned to her side.

On one of her trips, she spotted a calf stuck in the mud up to his sides. He was exhausted, his voice hoarse as he bawled for the cow that stood on the dried bank nearby.

T.J. surveyed the situation.

"Got to get him out some way. Glad I brought my rope along. Buddy, I'll try to catch him in my loop and we'll see if we can pull him out."

It took several tries for her to catch the calf's head.

"Now, let's see if Bess will back up and we can pull him out." She positioned herself at Bess' head and pushed back on the bridle reins as she spoke. "Back, back. That's a girl, keep going. Whoa! He's not coming, don't want to break his neck. Now what?"

She looked around for something to lay in the mud, so she could walk out to the calf. An old tree branch lay nearby.

"Pretty heavy. I'm not sure I can move that."

She struggled and finally dragged the branch to the

mud hole. Bess stood patiently with no tension on the rope.

T.J. wedged the branch under the calf's chest and pried.

She repositioned Bess for a straight pull to the front of the calf.

"Now, let's see if we can pull him up on that branch. Back, Bess, back."

The calf struggled, his front legs sucked out of the mud. When he came back down, he was astride the limb. T.J. eased Bess for a rest. The calf lay panting, exhausted by his struggles.

"Let's try again, easy now. Back Bess, back."

The calf's hind legs came out of the mud and he continued to struggle laying across the limb. His sides heaved. He gained enough strength to bawl.

His mother had lost interest in the hours he was trapped, but at his bawl, she came running.

"We've got to pull him the rest of the way out, but now we've got the cow to worry with. Back, Bess, let's pull him on out. He's choking, but he can get his breath when he hits dry ground. Back."

The calf slid across the mud slick and staggered up. His mother circled and the calf jumped up. The little animal staggered around the horse and the girl, tying them together. Buddy leaped into the tangle and his barking added to the irritation and fear of all the animals. The rope tightened with each move.

T.J. fell under Bess' hooves. The mare stopped, but with the struggling calf and her legs entangled, she was unable to manage her hooves as she would normally have done. All stood or lay where they were in their impasse. The calf tied, the mares legs tied, and T.J. under the mare, unable to crawl away. She reached for the stirrup above her head with her left hand; pulled and managed to get her hand into the pocket of her trousers.

"I've got a knife, if I can only get it out."

Buddy barked again. Everything tightened with his attack.

"Hush. Down boy, down." Buddy dropped and lay panting on his belly, ten feet from the cow, that eyed him suspiciously.

T.J. had the knife in her right hand.

How am I going to open it? I've got to let go of the stirrup.

"Steady, Bess, steady." She bent back her finger nail trying to open the knife, then used her teeth to straighten the blade.

Help me Lord. It won't matter where I cut the rope, if I can get some pressure off.

She sawed near Bess' leg where the rope was taunt and she could apply the most pressure. The rope unwound as she cut each of the big strands. She turned the blade away from Bess' leg to prevent an accident. The rope finally parted. It fell from Bess' legs. T.J. reached to flip the ends around to loosen the calf. The loop spread, the mud-slick calf walked through. He went directly to his mother and tried to nurse.

The old cow wasn't eager to linger, but tossed her head one last time and took off with the calf staggering close by her side.

T.J. shuddered and buried her face in her hands, mud and all.

She sat for several minutes recovering her strength. Buddy crept over and pried his nose into her hands. She hugged him to her, then reached up for Bess' stirrup. She pulled herself up, then stood with unsteady legs leaning on the mare's shoulder.

When she recovered her composure, she spoke, "We're a great team. Thank you Bess and Buddy, and thank you, Lord that we all came out of this safe."

She wiped her hands on the dry debris near the mud hole and then on her trousers. "Let's go home friends."

In sight of the shed, T.J. looked down at herself. *I can't see anyone like this. They'll wonder what happened. I'd be so embarrassed. I'll hurry and unsaddle, then get into the house before anyone sees me.*

Buddy ran ahead to the stock tank, got a drink, then climbed over the edge to cool off in the water. He splashed a moment, then climbed out and shook himself.

Jed came from the bunkhouse and looked toward the barns.

"Buddy, where's your mistress? She's been gone a long while today."

The dog lowered his head, looked away in an unsual manner.

Strange, he usually bounds to me with a welcome from his wet tongue.

The dog turned and went toward the barn, then turned, looked back once, and went into the cool shade. He flopped down on the clean straw and began to clean his paws.

Jed walked into the hallway, stopped, and looked down the cool center of the barn. When his eyes adjusted, he saw T.J. in a peculiar pose. He walked closer. She leaned on Bess.

His hand flew out automatically. He laid it on her shoulder, "T.J.?" He felt a tremor.

"Oh, I didn't see you. You crept up on me again." Her spine straightened, she turned her face toward the mare's shoulder and reached for the horn on the western saddle.

"Here, let me do that for you," Jed offered.

"I can take care of myself." Her voice was tight.

"I'm not busy now, please let me help you," Jed pleaded.

That was the last thing she wanted. T.J. jerked her face away quickly to hide the tears that started down her dirty cheeks. She couldn't hide the sob that erupted from her throat.

Jed dropped the saddle and reached for her shoulders. He spoke more gruffly than he intended, "What's the matter?"

"Nothing."

He pulled her shoulders around and looked squarely into her face. "You might as well tell me now, I'll find out anyway."

"Nothing! Nothing happened, can't you see. I'm muddy and I'm embarrassed, can't you just let it go?"

"No, tell me," he persisted.

"All right. You always want the last word. I tangled with an old cow and her calf. I got muddied in the process. They're fine and I'm fine. Now, let it go."

"You and Buddy certainly are muddy, she must have wallowed you in the mud," Jed said.

T.J. looked into his face to see if he knew the truth.

"Did you see us?" she asked.

He evaded. He hoped she'd give him more answers to his questions. "How'd it happen?"

T.J. looked at him and tried to pull away.

"Don't, T.J.! Just be honest and tell me this once." He

waited.

T.J.'s lip came out and her body stiffened.

"Answer me!" He shook her gently.

His action stayed her tears. "Why do you always have to be the boss?"

Jed's gaze slid to T.J.'s lips.

"You look like my baby brother used to look when he didn't get his way. You know how I got him over it?"

She stared at him.

"I tickled him and he'd get right over it,"

"Don't you dare!"

"Or, I ate his neck." He moved his head toward her neck.

She pulled away and he drew her toward him threateningly.

Her mouth flew open to answer, just before he landed his face at her neck. She struggled, then kicked his shin. Jed drew his head back to look into her face.

"There, at least that lip isn't sticking out anymore and by the way, that little kick was worth it." His grin thoroughly irritated T.J.

"You're taking advantage and I don't like that!" She spit through her teeth, then stepped further from Jed's reach.

Buddy planted himself between the pair with his lip drawn back, his eyes on Jed. A soft growl erupted from his throat.

"I'm sorry, I wouldn't have done that if you hadn't reminded me of my brother and how we used to act."

"Well, I hope your mother spanked the both of you!"

He turned away, a tired look entered his stance again.

"Sometimes she did. Go to the house, T.J. I'll clean up your mare and saddle."

It galled T.J., but she looked at his serious face and decided to flee the scene before emotions escalated out of control.

"Buddy, come." she turned and rushed toward the house with the dog at her side. *I can't run, but I want to.*

Later, Jed met Buddy in the path to the barn. He patted the dog and spoke, "Good dog. You take care of her, I can't."

He saddled his horse and back tracked T.J. to the watering hole. A rope end lay at the edge of the mudhole. Jed dismounted and pulled the rope from the mud. He fingered the cut end. It wasn't too hard to read the sign: *cow, calf, horse, and T.J.'s tracks; an animal bogged; someone roped it and got tangled, then had to cut the rope to release themselves; their horse, or dog. Which? Hard to tell, there are too many overlapping tracks.* A chill went over Jed. *It was a dangerous situation where someone could have been injured. I'll send someone with her next time besides the dog.*

He climbed aboard his buckskin and turned back toward headquarters. *More problems- always have to be so watchful.*

He looked out over the range where there should have been a waving stand of grass. Only short, dried pasture was left.

I love it here, but it's so unpredictable, two years of blizzards, now a drought. We can't hold on much longer, no matter who has some money stashed away. We have a little feed left in the ricks near the house, but there will be no hay cut here this year. May have to buy some before winter's over. Glad we sold those yearlings when it started getting dry. We drove them east, or we'd have been in even worse trouble. If we have blizzards again this year, I'm done. Sure hate to call it quits, but what can I do? I can't take T.J. and the rest down any further. I've got to find some way to pay her what I owe her.

Fourth of July Celebration

The whole crew went to town on Saturday. The ladies shopped at the general store for necessities, while the men lounged around talking with other hands.

"Rough times, you all still got a job?" one cowboy asked.

"Yeah, Jed's keepin' us on this summer," Max replied.

"We're plannin' on goin' up to the mountains to find some hay," Casey replied.

"Not much up there this year. We already been."

"Is that so?" Casey asked. "When did you go?"

"We got back yesterday."

"Bad year, think I'll move further east," another said.

"Yeah, 'bout given this territory enough of my life."

"Well, we'd kinda like to stick around, right, Max?" Casey asked.

"Yeah, let's walk on down by the saloon and see what's goin' on in there. Maybe they'll be more cheerful than you fellows." Max touched his hat and turned down the dusty track.

"Hope you find what you're lookin' for," one of the men called.

Max and Casey sauntered down the block.

"What's that sign on the wall there?" Max pointed.

"Looks like a Wild West show to me. Maybe that will give us a little excitement. Let's look it over."

The two men moved to the back of the crowd of cowhands who gathered near the sign.

"Read it out loud, will you?" hollered a dirty cowpoke.

"July Fourth Wild West Show. Horse races, wild horse ridin', wild cow milkin', ropin', and other contests. Here's the catch, ya gotta put up four bucks to enter any of the contests."

"That's next week."

"That's right. Anybody wanta bet I'll win the horse race?" A cowboy looked at the gathered crowd. No one took him up on his offer.

Several of the men turned away, quiet, figuring how they could raise four dollars to enter their choice of the contests.

Casey and Max sauntered across the street.

"The best deal would be the wild cow milkin', the team's only got to pay four bucks between three cowboys," Casey spoke softly in Max's ear. "With Jed and us, we could do that. Might even win."

"Yeah, let's go tell him," Max said.

"Jed, we want to talk to you," Casey signaled as the

bunch rode home behind the ladies' loaded buggy.

"What's on your mind?" Jed asked.

"Did you see the sign on the post office wall?"

"Were you boys thinking of entering one of the contests?" Jed asked.

"We can't afford much, but maybe between us, we three could scrape together four bucks. What'da you think, boss?"

"I'll go along with that. Who's the best bet, you two and me?"

"That'd be our choice," Max said.

"Fine, I'll come up with the money," Jed said.

"No, we'll kick in too. Only fair we all help out," Casey put in.

"Then, we'll split the take if we win," Jed replied. He twitched his reins and left the two.

"Where we comin' up with our part?" Max asked.

"I think Shaker will kick in, he's 'bout the only one of us ever got any money left over," Casey added.

"Yeah, think he'd like to be included. We'd divvy up with him, when we win," Max said.

"*When we win*, you're pretty certain are you?" Casey commented.

"We gotta be," Max said.

On the third, the three hands approached Jed. Shaker handed over the crumpled four dollars.

"Here's our wild cow milkin' entry fee."

Jed pushed Shaker's hand back. "I can't take the whole thing, I'll kick in my share."

Shaker pushed his hand out, "We got another idea, Boss."

"What's that?"

"Here's an extra two bucks, we want you to enter your buckskin in the horse race."

"I been thinking about that," Jed replied.

"She beats everything around, we think you'd win."

At supper on the evening of the third, Jed spoke to the ladies.

"We're gong to the show in town tomorrow. Me and the boys are planning on entering a few of the contests. If you ladies want to fix a picnic lunch, how about making a day of it?"

Mary looked at the excitement in T.J.'s eyes.

"Sure, we'd like to go, give us something exciting to do," T.J. replied as she turned away.

Mary looked sharply at T.J. *That girl has something bubbling in her brain already. What now? She's won a few races before, is she going to enter this time?*

The men left the house in a boisterous mood and T.J. went to her room. Mary followed. She tapped on the door. The girl opened it.

"T.J., what do you have on your mind?"

"Why do you think I have anything on my mind?"

"I've known you since before you were born, you can't fool me. Are you thinking about that race tomorrow?"

T.J. turned defiant eyes on Mary. "What if I am?"

"You know Jed is going to enter his buckskin, don't you?"

"That's fine, we can be first and second, no problem."

"Who is going to be first?" Mary asked.

"Me, of course!" T.J. crowed.

"Don't be so sure, haven't you learned anything on this ranch? You don't always win and you shouldn't," Mary stated.

"May the *best man* win. That's what I always say," T.J. boasted.

"You and Jed have made some progress, do you want to ruin all that? We all have to live here, don't forget," Mary stated.

"I won't. The ranch needs the money, that's all I'm thinking about," T.J. said.

"Sure, you are. I know how competitive you are. I'm sorry, but you haven't convinced me that you'll do the right thing. Will you please pray about it and think of someone else for a change?"

"Fine! I'll pray about it, but I'm still going to do it."

"T.J., use your hard head for once, instead of your heart. You aren't quite in the state God wishes for you, or you wouldn't answer *before* God speaks to you."

"I said, I'd pray about it, didn't I?" T.J. said.

"Attitude, attitude," Mary shook her head.

All afternoon, Mary found T.J. very quiet. The young woman left the house at dusk, carrying a saddle bag. Mary looked out the kitchen window and saw her go into the shed where the saddles were kept.

Oh, Lord, help that girl. She's too much for me to manage. I'm proud of her. I know my brother would be too, but she's hard on herself and everyone else. Give Jed the patience to deal with her too. I think they really care for each other, but neither one will give in. It's in your hands, I'm not strong enough. I don't know what to do next. Wish Roy or her daddy were here.

Mary brushed a tear from her cheek and turned to straighten the dishtowel.

The ladies rose at five and began to fry chickens.

Mary commented, "Just like the old fashioned church picnics we used to go to when we lived further east."

T.J. danced around. "Yes, I haven't been to a really big celebration in a long time. This is going to be fun."

"I sure *hope* so," Mary said.

T.J. grinned. "Where's your faith, Auntie?"

The men were dressed in their more rugged clothes to participate in the cow milking contest.

Each team was assigned a particular cow. Jed and the two hands drew a brindle with one horn growing down over her right eye.

The teams lined up across a line in the dirt of the corral. The cows stirred nervously in the pen at the far end.

A judge explained, "We'll turn loose all the cows at once, each of the teams have their assigned cow. Catch her anyway you can and the first one to bring back enough milk to *pour*, I'd better say *drip*, out of their whiskey bottle is the winner. You boys ready?"

"Whoa," Jed hollered. "Where do we take the milk?"

"Sorry, guess I forgot to tell you that."

The contestants hooted.

"Right here to the starting line. The banker and I'll be standing here, I mean *over that gate* waiting. Any more questions?"

A spectator called, "Why don't you stand in the corral?"

"No thanks, I think it may be a little more fair to stand on the other side of this gate. Come on Mr. Oliver. Come on through and we'll start these fellows out."

The teams lined up, strategy discussed while they waited.

"On your mark, ready, set, go!"

The cows bolted from the pen when the men shouted on their end. The cows ran toward the men, broke apart and moved in all directions.

Jed and the boys had stayed together, all aimed at their brindle cow. Another old cow stopped in their path and pawed the earth. Her team jumped at her and Jed's bunch flowed by.

Casey yelled, "Hurry, fellows. I got her tail, grab her head!"

Jed leaped for her head and wrapped one gloved hand around her crooked horn. She stepped on his toe. He lost his footing and his hold when she tossed her head into his lower chest. He leaned into her and pulled his foot from under her shifting hoof.

Casey hung on to her swinging rear end while Max tried to grab a teat. He got hold and moved with her as she swung away from him. She ran ahead, dragging Casey and Jed with her. Jed twisted her head and she came against the corral fence.

"Now, get it!" he yelled.

Max took two squeezes and ran for the judges, along with several other cowboys.

Jed yelled at Casey, "Don't let her go yet, just in case he didn't get enough."

"She ain't bad now, we got her broke," Casey laughed.

"Or she's got us broke, one," Jed laughed from his position at the cow's head.

Cows continued to run over men. Several bumped into Jed and Casey. Some hands got up from the dust and continued their pursuit. The crowd yelled encouragement and jeers, depending on who they rooted for.

The milkers began lining up in front of the judges. Max was second in line. The crowd screamed as the judges attempted to pour milk from the first bottle. *Nothing!* The judge held his hand under the neck to catch any possible drips.

"Gotta be fair, here, give the banker your bottle and let's see if you got any."

Max handed his bottle to Cleveland Oliver. The banker pretended to slosh the liquid in the bottle. He took off his glove and held his hand palm up. Dramatically, he tipped the bottle and watched as milk coated the inside of the bottle. He waited, the crowd jeered. Two drops dripped onto his hand. He raised Max's hand in a boxer's victory stanch and the crowd went wild.

Several of the fence standing cowboys threw up their hats in salute and one man threw his hat on the ground and stomped away.

Cowboys in the corral began to dust themselves off and retrieve their hats.

"Ready, let her go." Jed released the brindle cow's head and Casey the tail at almost the same moment. She shook her head and ran off with her tail over her back.

Several of the cowboys helped their team mates up out of the dirt. Three limped off.

Jed slapped Casey on the back. "Good job. None of us hurt, that's good."

"We did it!" Casey ran to congratulate Max.

The judges awarded the second, third, and fourth place prizes.

Jed picked Mary and T.J. out of the crowd and saluted them with his thumb in the air. The two smiled and clapped.

After the three collected congratulations, Jed looked back and didn't see the ladies in the crowd. He caught Casey's arm. "Check on the ladies will you? I've got to go get my horse ready for the race."

"Sure, Boss." Jed watched as Casey and Max walked around the outside of the fence.

Inside the ring, horsemen attempted to drive the cows from the corral and back into the smaller pen. Some animals seemed reluctant to go. The crowd stirred restlessly, awaiting the big race.

A few firecrackers went off. The cows threw their heads in the air and hurried back into the pen.

One horse bucked in fright at all the confusion. The crowd cheered when the cowboy stayed on and brought his animal under control. He doffed his hat and bowed to their applause.

Horses began to arrive for the race.

Shaker looked over the animals, trying to see Jed and the buckskin.

Mary came to his side.

Shaker glanced her way, "They're lookin' good. Sure hope he wins, we need that prize for winter feed."

"Yes, but mostly, please just keep them safe," Mary pled.

"Yes, that too." He turned to look beyond Mary. "Where's T.J.?"

Mary looked away, "She'll be along soon."

"She's not pullin' somethin' is she?" Shaker questioned.

"I hope not."

Max and Casey came up. "Hello, where's T.J.?"

Mary didn't answer.

"Jed sent us to keep you ladies company, where is she?"

Mary was saved answering by a cheer from the crowd. A number of horses swept into the corral and rode around the edges. The cheers followed them around the fence.

Mr. Oliver held up his hand for silence.

"Exactly thirty seconds and this race will be under way. Listen carefully to the directions. We have judges stationed around the course. The rules state: no whipping anyone else's horse; horse and rider must pass between the flags at all times; riders must be mounted at the finish line, which is the same as the starting line. If anyone breaks the rules, that judge has the obligation to disqualify any rider he catches not abiding by the rules. He won't stop the race, but that rider will be disqualified at the end of the race. A winner will not be declared until all judges report in."

"Riders, come by single file and get your numbers. Wear them around your neck in plain sight on your backs. The judges have to be able to see your number. Ride by when you get your numbers on and let us see you."

"Take it easy boys, we got plenty of time, don't crowd."

Some helped others with their numbers until the judges were satisfied that all the riders were easily identified. The judges stood thirty feet apart and called the riders to come between them. One whole side of the corral had been opened to allow plenty of room for the horses to leave the corral in one long front.

"Settle your horses. There, Mr. Jones, calm that animal down. We can't have him rearing and kicking everything in sight. Tom, move up. Jones, move your sorrel back two feet."

"If we have a false start, I'll fire the pistol again. You'll all have to come back. This has got to be a fair start, we don't want to call you back and you won't want to come. Careful there, settle down."

"Jones, stop abusing that animal or you'll be disqualified before we start. You'll all ride between the flags or you're out of the race."

A bay horse stayed on the outside with a small man aboard.

Jed sat his buckskin, alert, but calm, three from the far end.

He looked down the line. Most of the horses were somewhat thin, due to the drought. Jed had considered if it was fair for him to use his mare in this extra effort, but balanced the additional feed they could afford against the few minutes of extreme effort.

Lord, I hope I'm doing the right think for the whole ranch. Keep everyone safe, make it a good race for all.

The starter raised his blank pistol. "Ready, set- ,"he fired the pistol.

The animals surged forward, all getting a balanced start, except for Jones and his plunging stallion. The man laid on his whip and the horse leaped forward.

Shaker commented, "That should be a good horse, but that man's got him almost crazy. Sure hope he don't run over somebody."

Mary had her knuckles in her mouth in a pained expression. There wasn't much for them to do for the next five minutes but listen to the sounds as the race advanced though the main street, then around the town and back toward the corral.

Mary turned as the sounds moved. They could follow the movement by the noise of the viewers. Some ran to peep through the buildings to see the horses coming or leaving the next areas. Others stood on the roofs of the buildings and gave a running commentary.

"There's a horse down. That horse jumped clear over it. A bay is down too, it tripped right over that downed rider."

"There goes one off the track, it's running away. The rider can't get it back on the track. Whoops, it ran into a bush and it's up and going again. The rider is barely hanging on. There, he's off and his horse is running on. I can't see them anymore, they've all gone around the corner."

Mary stood with her eyes closed. *Please God, don't let anyone be hurt or the horses, please.*

Shaker took her arm. "Miss Mary, are you all right?"

"I hope so." She looked into his face. "I'm afraid. Shaker, T.J. is riding in that race too. What if she gets hurt, I'll never forgive myself for not telling Jed beforehand."

"You think he could have stopped her?" Shaker commented.

"Not really. No one's ever been able to keep her from doing what she wanted to do," Mary said.

"Well, here they come. I can see the dust. Step up on my knee and you can see them coming." Shaker linked his hands on his bent knee. Mary put one hand on his shoulder and stepped up.

Head above the crowd, she saw Jed's buckskin in front with a herd of horses right behind him. "I can't see T.J!"

"It's hard to tell from this angle, they'll soon be abreast of us, then we can tell."

Mary leaned over. "Let me down, I can see now."

Shaker straightened in time to see the horses flow by. "Jed won, didn't he?"

"I think so," Mary answered.

The judges began to gather from the further reaches of the race. They conferred.

Banker Oliver cleared his throat. "We have a winner. Mr. Jed Snowden! Here you go on the buckskin."

Jed rode forward and saluted with his hat.

Mr. Oliver turned to the other judges. "And our second place winner is T. Smith on the bay." he looked at the young rider who came forward.

His mouth gaped open, "T.J., is that you?"

T.J. rode forward and removed her hat. Her hair fell in strands from the bun atop her head.

"Ladies and gentlemen, we have a lady as our second place winner!"

Jones screamed, "Ain't no women s'posed to be ridin' in this race!"

Banker Oliver turned to the other judges. They put their heads together and went into conference.

"Ladies and gentlemen, may I have your attention? Our rules speak nothing of gender, T.J. is our second place winner. She won it fair and square."

"Hip, hip, hooray for Miss Smith."

Jones spit and swore.

"Be a good sport!"

"A lady beat you, good enough for you."

"That'll take you down a peg," came from the crowd.

Jones came forward to accept his third place prize and rode sullenly out of the corral.

Jed stepped off his buckskin, pulled the reins over her head, loosened the saddle cinch, and walked her away with his head down.

T.J. wished she knew what he was thinking. She looked for Mary and gave her a tentative smile.

Mary frowned and signaled for T.J. to meet them at their buggy.

Max and Casey slapped each other on the back.

"Did you ever?"

"No, I didn't. I didn't know she could do that, but I knew she was a good rider," Casey said.

"Yeah, we saw that on our trail drive two springs ago," Max replied.

Shaker shook his head as he walked along beside Miss Mary.

Mary twisted her gloves in her hand and kept silent.

After the contestants collected their prize money and ate their silent lunch, Jed, T.J., Mary, and Shaker, rode home without a word.

Max and Casey became subdued after several attempts at celebration.

The next day in the shed, T.J. confronted Jed. "Well, you might as well say it, I know you're going to. Let's get it over with."

"What can I say, T.J.? You're a grown woman. No matter what I wish, you're going to do what you want to, I can't stop you. Guess I ought to know that by now."

"I would like your approval," she said.

He answered, "I did it for winter feed, what did you do it for?"

"I did it for the ranch too."

"I can't question another's motives, but you need to think before you act."

T.J. spoke, "I added my winnings to the ranch funds, it will go for winter feed for the stock."

Jed lowered his head. "I can't be proud and turn any legitimate funds down. The Lord knows we are going to need it." He turned his head aside and looked away. His voice caught, "Your mare was abreast of me, but T.J. do you know how close you came to going down when you jumped that horse? I never thought you could stay up."

Jed's emotion touched her, but she covered. "I couldn't stop, there was no other choice, go down or jump, and Bess did it."

"Yes, she did. She's a remarkable little animal. I didn't know she had it in her."

"We've jumped before- maybe, not that far," she replied.

"Please be careful, if something happened to you- anyone on this ranch-   I'd-   we'd all feel very guilty and never forgive ourselves."

"I know, Jed. I'm sorry, I'll try to be a little more thoughtful next time."

"I wish you could." He hated the disappointment on her face. Seeking to remove it, he searched his memory.

"By the way, since the race, I've got your and Mary's hundred dollars for your pay this year."

"We don't need it."

"I know, but I owe it and I pay my debts. For once, just agree and do what we said we would," Jed said.

"All right." T.J. smiled.

He was surprised by her agreeable manner.

He turned and walked toward the door.

T.J. fell in beside him. She skipped to keep up with his long stride.

"It was fun though. I might have won if that horse hadn't slipped."

He whirled toward her, "T.J.!"

She grinned and walked off toward the ranch house.

Jed watched her go, a mixture of admiration and anger on his face. He brushed his hand across his face and groaned.

Fencing

Jed gathered the hands, T.J., and Mary around the supper table.

"We need to think about fencing our range in the next year or two. We'll start putting in posts on the boundaries this next spring and work in our spare time. We'll bring in posts and barbed wire by train and haul them by wagon to the ranch."

"Ain't that wire gonna cut up the cows? We'll have a screw worm epidemic on our hands with all those wire cuts," Max said.

Jed pushed his hat around on his knee. "It's possible, but it's going to be required to hold the homestead. We'll have to take our chances and hope the stock learns real quick what the fences are for. I hope they'll stay out of them. They say where fences are used the cows stay out of them after a few weeks. Our Missouri cows should already know about fences, even though theirs were mostly wooden fences."

Jed continued, " It will add another job, we'll have to ride the fences to keep them in place. We check the stock fairly often. We'll carry our lariats and continue to have a bottle of screw worm medicine in every hand's saddle bag."

"It'll probably add a few more hours to all our work

load, but in another way, we won't be dividing stock or looking for strays so much, they should stay on our own range, if we do a good job on keeping the fences up. I'll go out with you and we'll all learn how to build fence."

"I'll pick up the tools we'll need when I get the posts and wire," Jed finished.

"I ain't excited about buildin' fence, but guess that's part of the job from here on out," Casey said.

"Things do change and open range is becoming an old way of life. It'll be different, but we'll get used to it," Jed rose.

"Thanks ladies, guess it's time to hit the hay." He turned, "Night."

The other men rose and left the house.

T.J. and Mary picked up the last dishes, straightened the chairs, and wiped off the table.

"Mary, I'll wash," T.J. said.

"Things sure are changing," Mary said. "Hope it's for the best."

"It's going to cost a few dollars again. Glad we've got a couple of years to get it all done," T.J. said.

The Wild Cow Milkers

Jed and Shaker watched the ladies turn the old cow out from their morning milking.

"That old milk cow sure is getting some age on her. She can't hardly walk nomore," Shaker commented.

"We've got two good heifer calves out of her. Sure was glad when we could buy her from the homestead on the next place," Jed added.

"They said they put her in the soddy with them during the blizzards. Helped keep 'em warm and her alive," Shaker said.

'She was the last cow they had when they pulled up stakes. Glad we could get her. She's served us well. Wish her oldest heifer was old enough to milk, but we'll have to wait until at least next spring."

"That old 'un ain't gonna make it till spring," Shaker commented.

"Jed shook his head, "Shaker, we've got to get rid of that old cow before she dies. Do you think you could drive her to the butcher on Friday?"

"I don't know if she can make the miles or not," Shaker scratched his throat under his chin stubble.

"T.J. likes her. I hate to see her die on the place," Jed said.

T.J. stepped around the corner. "No, you can't sell her to the butcher. She's earned the right to die right here."

Shaker ducked and moved off toward the bunk house. He muttered to himself when he was out of earshot, "This is one discussion I don't need."

Jed pushed his hat back on his head. "That's ranch life, T.J. She' can't handle another winter!"

"I don't care, she may have outlived her usefulness, but she's earned her right to a peaceful death, right here where she's supported us for almost the last two years."

"Think it over T.J., we've had two winters of blizzards and now a drought. We don't have pasture for anything that can't pay it's own way."

Jed turned on his heel and moved to his buckskin. He stepped aboard and squeezed his left knee. The mare stepped off, then broke into a canter toward the hills to the west.

T.J. watched him go, then turned to the soft-eyed old cow. She stroked the blaze between the old girl's eyes.

"Just an old lady." She rubbed harder and the old cow closed her eyes. "You've sure been a good one. Your two girls are out there growing. They'll make good cows before too much longer. I won't let them butcher you." She gave a final pat and turned from the pasture.

One week later, from inside the house, T.J. and Mary heard a bawl outside in the road. The ladies looked out to see Max dragging a cow with a lariat around her horns. Foam dripped from the cow's open mouth. A small calf tagged along behind.

Casey followed encouraging the calf along with a flip

of his lariat, then he bounded ahead to open the pasture gate. The two men caught the calf; shoved him into the shed; and closed the gate.

T.J. and Mary followed and leaned over the gate. "What you got there?" the young woman asked.

"Miss T.J., Jed said to bring you this new milk cow and for us to lock the calf in the barn, so you can milk her in the morning."

"Is she broke to milk? She looks like a young cow," Mary observed.

"No, she ain't 'xactly broke yet, but we'll help you, come mornin'."

In the morning, Max held the calf while Casey drove the cow under the shed. He crowded her up against the wall and roped her to an upright post. She resisted their efforts to settle her. With her head down, she bucked and kicked out with her hind leg whenever they came near. Forward or backward, she was handy with her kicks.

"Turn the calf loose, I'll crowd in while he nurses!" Casey set himself up as closely as he dared to the cow's udder with a small bucket in one hand.

"She probably won't give much today, we've treated her too rough," Max observed.

T.J. and Mary watched as the men jumped around, avoiding the hooves and the twisting cow.

"We gotta put kickers on her!" Casey said. "Grab her tail and push her over against the wall."

Casey grabbed a pair of metal u-shaped irons hooked together with a short chain. "Hang on, I'm gonna put these on."

The hungry calf moved toward its mother and Casey stayed on the down side.

"There, I got her hocks. You can turn her tail loose now and step back. Let's see what she does now."

The cow continued to struggle, but she couldn't do much.

"She's trussed up like a Christmas goose, come on and get her milked, Max."

"I thought you was gonna do that?"

"I'll keep my hand on her hip, get it done before that calf finishes," Casey grunted.

Each day, the struggle continued, the results hardly worth the effort. A scant half gallon of milk was the yield each day.

After a month of the ladies milking the old cow and the men assisting with the new cow, the hands declared her ready for the ladies to try.

"Let's see how you do today with us watching. If you have trouble, we'll help."

Mary and T.J. were not sure.

Mary remarked, "Well, *we are not* and *don't intend to be* a wild cow milking team, but if you boys say so, here goes."

"I thought you was gonna do that," Casey said.

Strangely, the cow seemed more settled with the ladies and it looked as if she was finally broken for milking.

"Guess you've got a lighter hand, she seems better with you two," Max commented.

"I think you two can be milkmaid to her from now on," Casey replied.

"If you get into trouble, let us know and we'll help again."

The two men pulled their hats down snug and walked

off.

Mary looked after them. "You know, I think they're relieved. Don't believe they liked doing our jobs."

"I think you're right. Guess this is women's work," T.J. said.

Summer progressed and temperatures began to drop with the advent of fall. T.J. took a hard cold and coughed for a week. She shivered from fever.

"T.J., you're getting worse, if you don't take care of yourself, you're going to have pneumonia," Mary said.

"No, I can help. It's too much for you to do all the outside work yourself. It does me good to get a little fresh air every day," she coughed.

Rain came that afternoon, dampness seeped into the ground and hung in the air. Mary insisted T.J. stay inside and warm.

"All right, just this once. But if you need anything, hit the dinner ring and I'll wrap up good and be out to help you."

Mary pulled on her old coat and put a shawl over her head.

"I should be back in about half an hour. The stew may need a little stir and more water if I don't get along as fast by myself as the two of us. Sit here by the fireplace and use this blanket to cover up. I'll be back soon."

T.J. settled in. The cozy warmth made her drowsy.

She woke with a start when she heard a sizzle from the fireplace. She raised herself and reached for the heavy iron pot.

"I'll put in some water. That will be just right by the time Mary comes in." She took the dipper from the bucket and added water. She glanced out the window.

The cows are still in the shed. It's getting darker outside. It must be the rain, or I dozed off.

She walked to the door and looked out.

She called, "Mary? Mary? Are you getting along all right?" She listened. *Nothing stirring out here. I'll give her another minute, then I'll check.*

She reached for her work coat and wool shawl to pull over her head. She turned and paced the floor and then resolutely opened the door.

Hurriedly, she walked toward the shed. She heard a bellow, her heart caught for an instant.

T.J. broke into a run.

"Mary?" She peered over the gate. The old cow stood on one wall, the calf peeped from behind her. Mary hung high on the back wall with her fingers clutching a cross beam. She was bent at an odd angle.

At T.J.'s voice, the young cow turned toward the gate. A rope hung from her neck and foam from her jaw. She bellowed, then hit the gate at T.J.'s waist.

T.J. jerked away from the gate, then heard a soft moan.

"Mary, I'm here. Are you all right?"

"She won't let me down," Mary gasped.

I've got to get Mary out of there. "I'll open the gate and let her out. Maybe with the calf and the old cow, she'll go on and I can get to you."

Mary spoke with a gasp. "Don't let her get you. She's upset and she might knock you down." She hesitated, "You'll have to get behind the gate."

T.J. went to the latch, started to lift the bar. The cow hit the gate again, then stood shaking the whole gate with her head. Her long horns caught and held before she jerked free and hit up and down the slates.

"She's crazy," T.J. commented.

"Yes, and she can hurt you too."

"Mary, are you hurt?"

"Yes-   She got me in the ribs and bruised my leg when I tried to go up the wall."

"How did she get loose?"

"I guess the rope broke."

"I've got to figure out how to get you out of there," T.J. touched the gate again. The cow lunged into the slates at her hands.

"She's totally berserk, I don't know how you are going to get her out without her hurting one of us," Mary groaned.

T.J. tried several methods and each time the cow acted more crazed. She looked at the pasture, where the horses should be. None were there or in sight. None of the men were around and Buddy had gone with them.

I feel faint, can't walk a long way to catch a horse. Mary's hurt and can't run.

Bent double, she coughed.

She looked back into the shed, Mary sagged more and more down the wall. Each time her foot slipped, the cow turned to threaten her.

"I can't hold on much longer," Mary sobbed.

T.J. rattled the gate again.

"Get the cow away, I'm going to fall," Mary whispered.

T.J. made a quick decision, "Hang on, I'm going after the rifle."

When T.J. disappeared from the gate, Mary cried softly. Her predicament become more and more perilous by the moment.

Without T.J.'s distraction, the cow turned toward Mary. The crazed cow caught Mary's foot and thrashed it against the wall. Mary groaned and clung with her numb fingers.

"Oh, God help me!"

T.J. stumbled toward the house. She grabbed the rifle from above the mantle. Shells were in the gun for emerencies.

She went onto the porch, levered a shell into the chamber and ran toward the shed.

As she rounded the end, the cow hit the wall at her aunt's foot again. Mary moaned and slipped.

T.J. threw off the rifle safety and rattled the gate.

The cow lunged toward her. T.J. stuck the muzzle through the gate, aimed and pulled the trigger. She levered another shell into the gun in one smooth motion.

The maddened cow kept coming, hit the gate. The boards snapped open, hit T.J. in the chest and sent her flying. She sprawled where she landed, pinned by the weight of the gate.

Catching her breath brought a spasm of coughing. The cow turned back toward the sound and struck, hooking the gate, then brought her horns toward the girl in a frenzy.

T.J. fired the chambered shell, point blank. The cow

sank to her knees; rolled to her side; and hooked one final time. She hit T.J. on the forehead with a horn in her final convulsive move.

The spent opponents slipped away into a deathly silence.

T.J. didn't see Mary slide down the wall and land in a heap.

The calf fled the gate and ran across the pasture. The older cow shuffled out the gate and crippled off toward the pasture and its damp, but dead grass.

Forty five minutes later, the men rode in. The first thing they saw was the calf in the pasture.

"Strange the women let that calf out," Max commented.

Jed looked toward the shed. "T.J. was sick, I don't think she let it out." His face turned grim and he bumped his buckskin with his heel; rounded the shed; and leaped from the saddle.

He saw the gleam of the rifle barrel by a dark bundle pinned to the ground by the gate. The bundle didn't move. The young cow lay stretched across the door sill a foot from the still bundle.

"T.J., are you all right?" He lifted the gate, then pulled the shawl from her face. There was no movement. He heard a moan from the shed.

The men had followed their boss more slowly. Max took in the situation and moved toward the crumpled woman in the shed.

"Miss Mary?"

She groaned.

"We got real trouble, Boss."

"At least Mary's still alive," Casey commented.

Mary managed to whisper, "Help T.J., I haven't heard her since the cow broke out. Is she here?"

"She's here, but she's unconscious," Jed spoke grimly.

"Be careful, don't hurt her more," Mary managed to direct.

Jed came alive. "Get blankets and a door from inside the house. We've got to get them inside out of this damp."

Casey and Max hurried to the house. The men ran up the stairs. One grabbed blankets from the upstairs bedrooms while the other removed the hinge pins from the door.

When they returned to the barn, Jed took over.

"Get T.J. first," Mary moaned.

He laid the door beside T.J. and covered it with a blanket.

"Men, we've got to move her all together, we don't want to hurt her anymore. Casey, you get at her head, I've got her body and feet. Max, we'll roll her up, you push the door under her. Easy now."

The men moved in unison. They had moved injured cowpokes before.

Jed covered T.J. with a blanket.

"Now, pick up the door and let's get her inside."

The men moved toward the porch.

"Careful, turn it just a little. There, we're through. Put her in front of the fireplace. We've got to be sure she's warm enough."

Casey shuffled his feet, "Boss, I think Max and me

better get back and help Mary."

"Yes, take the other bedroom door and carry her in. I don't want to move T.J. again." Jed turned back. In the firelight, a dark bruise stood out on her forehead, dried blood extended from her nose down one cheek. Her breathing was shallow, but even.

"Oh, God, please don't let her die." He heard the stew sizzle, reached and pushed the pot back away from the heat. He rose, poured water into another pot and placed it in the fireplace coals.

While he waited, he looked at T.J., then wiped his eyes with the back of his hand.

"Here's Mary," Max said.

"What are we going to do?" Casey asked.

"I think one of you better go for the doctor. Max, you're the lightest, go as quick as you can. Remember the short cut is closed. It's dark, don't take chances, you need to get there. Take my buckskin."

"Sure, Boss." Max pulled his slicker tighter on his frame and left the house at a run.

Casey rubbed his hand over his face. "Now, what are we gonna do?"

Jed turned, "Get Shaker, he's the best doctor we've got until the real one comes."

"All right, I'll have him back here as soon as I can."

"Shoot three times when you get out about a mile. He was bringing in the supply wagon, so he shouldn't be more'n a mile or two out by now."

"Yeah, he'll probably meet me half way," Casey turned and hurried out the door, his slicker flapping.

Jed laid a cool cloth on the bump above T.J.'s eye. She didn't move.

The house was so quiet, Jed moved to Mary.

"Mary?"

"Ye- es."

"How are you doing?"

"I think I'll be fine. The cow must have- broken a few ribs. She got my foot. How's T.J.?" Mary closed her eyes.

"I'm not sure, she's still unconscious," Jed reached for a cloth and wrung it out. He laid it on Mary's forehead.

"She saved me," Mary whispered. "She can't be bad hurt. Oh, God, please take care of T.J." Mary raised her hand to the cloth and turned on her side, "Oh."

"Easy, easy." Jed covered her with a dry blanket. "Yes, she's got to be all right."

He turned and knelt on one knee by the younger woman. He reached for the wet cloth on T.J.'s face, turned to the cool side, and replaced it on her forehead. He wrung another and gently wiped the dried blood from her cheek.

I got to be patient. Lord, take care of these women. Please don't let them really be hurt.

He rested his chin on his upraised knee and watched the rise and fall of T.J.'s chest.

Mary finally spoke, "You know that old cow saved my life tonight."

"How's that," Jed asked.

"When the young cow broke loose and first hit me, I was able to use the old cow for a shield long enough to reach the back wall. If it hadn't been for her, I don't think I could have made it. That new cow went after anything that moved."

"The old cow's a good one," Jed spoke softly.

"I'm grateful to her," Mary breathed, "and to God."

Shaker and Casey arrived, but very little was left for them to do. Casey went back outside and Shaker puttered around putting supplies away.

Doctor Andrew's fast trotter kept pace with Jed's worn buckskin. The two slid into the yard an hour after midnight.

After a quick survey, the doctor directed the men.

"T.J.'s fine for the moment. She won't wake up for a time, so let's take Mary to her bedroom and I'll tend to her."

The three men carried Mary up the narrow stairs on the door and placed her gently on her bed. Mary groaned when they moved quickly.

"Sorry, Ma'am, we're sorry," Max apologized.

Dr. Andrews spoke when she was on the bed. "Fine, now you fellows can go on."

Jed returned to T.J.'s side.

Max and Casey drifted off toward the bunk house. They stopped to cool off the two worn horses and put them in the shed for a good feed of oats.

"Guess we better butcher out that cow," Casey said.

"Yeah, her meat may be tough, stirred up like that, but the Boss won't want it to go to waste. Better get at it," Max agreed.

Dr. Andrews spoke in a soothing voice, "Mary, where are you hurt?"

"My ribs and my right limb."

"I'll try not to hurt you. Shall we get you out of some of these clothes?" He gently loosened her dress and laid aside her damp outer clothing. He probed the bruises along Mary's rib cage and side.

"The best I can do for your ribs is to bind them up. Can you lean forward?"

"Humph- "

Dr. Andrews proceeded efficiently, winding white cloth around and round Mary's ribcage over her camisole.

"There, think that's taken care of. That should support you. Now let me see that limb."

He rolled off her stocking, probed the foot, went up the ankle and side of Mary's leg. He frowned, "Not much I can do here, lots of bruising and your ankle is badly sprained. Don't think anything's broken. You'll need to keep your leg up and stay off it for a few days. I'll put these pillows under your knee and foot, then I'll wrap the ankle too. That will keep down some of the swelling until you can start to heal."

He turned aside to remove a packet from his bag. He mixed a powder into the glass of water on her bed table.

"Here, drink this," he directed.

"Hand me my robe off the back of that chair."

The doctor assisted her into the robe, then laid her back carefully on her pillow.

Mary caught her breath.

He covered her with a quilt, pulling the weight up off her injured foot.

"Now, you're set. I'll get one of the fellows to sit here, in case you need anything more. I'll be downstairs, call if your pain gets too bad or anything else occurs."

"No, you don't need to send anyone up," Mary

protested.

"Yes, I do. I need to stay with T.J. and you may need more pain medicine or a drink during the night. Don't try to get up by yourself, a rib might puncture your lung. If you have to get up, let someone lift you to a sitting position. I'll send Shaker up, he's a good nurse." The doctor smiled.

He patted her shoulder, snapped his bag closed and walked to the door. He looked back, but Mary had her eyes closed. Her face was pale and pinched with pain.

The doctor walked quietly down the stairs to keep vigil by T.J.'s pallet.

"Shaker, you go up and sit with Mary for now. I've given her pain medication and she should sleep soon. Don't let her get up by herself and call me if she is in too much pain"

Buddy lay before the fire and as close to T.J. as Jed allowed.

The doctor spent most of the night in the rocking chair with a quilt over himself.

Jed lay on the rug near T.J.

During the restless night, he wished he could take her into his arms and heal her hurts.

Near dawn, T.J. began to moan and make sounds. She tossed restlessly.

"Can't you do something?" Jed asked Dr. Andrews.

"Not yet. She's trying to wake up and I've got to see what her problems are before I decide what to do next. I'll be here, maybe it would be easier if you weren't."

"Sorry," Jed apologized. "It's so hard to sit by and do nothing."

"I know, but often patience is the best medicine. Doctors take a vow to do no harm and sometimes doing nothing is the best. I know it's hard to see someone you love suffer."

"Yes, but I'm not leaving until she's better," Jed said.

In another hour, T.J. slipped into a more peaceful sleep.

Dr. Andrews awoke several hours later.

"She's better. She'll rest now, that's what she needs most. I'll step outside for a moment, then you'd better take a break." The good doctor rose to stretch.

No one saw Jed take T.J.'s hand and raise it to his lips. He kept that position. He offered the latest of his many prayers. "Dear Father, Thank you for sparing T.J. and Mary. Please heal their bodies and relieve their pain. I love them, Lord, you know that. They're family. Please take care of them. Thank you, Lord."

When Doctor Andrews returned, he nodded. Jed left T.J.'s side and quietly stepped to the porch. He rubbed his hand over his face and the stubble on his jaw.

When he looked, the rising sun revealed a dark shadow laying in the pasture near where the calf rested.

"What now?" Jed walked through the gate and by the shed. Max and Casey had finished dressing out the young cow last evening. The sides hung from the rafters where Mary had clung before.

"Boss, it was cold last night. The cow had bled out good, so we salvaged what we could.," Max said.

"Thanks."

Jed picked up the rifle, emptied the spent cartridge

onto the ground, retrieved it. He levered the unused shells into his hand. Thumped the barrel of the rifle against the heel of his boot twice, then wiped it with his bandanna. He looked down the barrel at the open chamber, then walked to the shadow in the pasture.

The old cow lay stretched on her side with a great gash in her flank. She grunted in pain with each breath and weakly raised her head when he moved around her. Jed knelt by her head and lay his hand on her neck.

"Thanks, old girl. I'm glad T.J. didn't let me sell you. You did the best you could, now the best I can do is put you out of your misery."

Jed levered the chamber closed, opened it, then inserted one shell. He held the muzzle a foot from the blaze in the center of her forehead.

"Good-by." He pulled the trigger. The cow never twitched.

In the house, both ladies jerked.

T.J. tried to speak and then got out, "Mary? Where's Mary?"

Dr. Andrews lay his hand on her arm and soothed her. "Mary's fine. She's upstairs in her own bed resting. You'll be fine too, when you've had a little time. Let me see your eyes." He held the lantern with his free hand and gazed into T.J.'s eyes. "Fine, rest now. Sleep."

"Jed?"

He's outside right now, but he's been here right by your side all night. Rest now. He'll be back soon."

T.J. drifted off again into a restless sleep.

Jed hitched the team to the sled. He pulled along side of the old cow's body. The hands helped him roll her up onto the platform.

He spoke to Max and Casey, "I don't want T.J. to be reminded of this ordeal when she recovers."

He drove the team with the sled toward the hills where he disposed of the carcass.

Jed returned to the front porch, cleaned the rifle, opened the door and strolled to the fireplace. He restored the rifle to its place over the mantel.

T.J. awoke when she heard the click of its replacement.

"Jed?"

"Yes, T.J., I'm glad you're awake. Are you better?"

"I'm sore all over, but I think I'll be fine." She was quiet for a moment. "Did I hear a shot?"

Jed couldn't answer.

"Jed?"

"I'm here, T.J." He reached for her hand.

"Did I hear a shot?

"Yes."

"What was it?"

"I had to take care of something."

"What?"

His voice was gruff, "Let it go, T.J. I'll tell you about it later."

"Was it our old cow?" she whispered.

"What makes you think that?" Jed hedged.

"I saw her."

"I'm sorry. It was the only merciful thing to do," he

replied.

"I know." She was quiet again. "If she'd only been younger." T.J. turned to her side and faced the fire with her eyes closed.

Jed watched her for a moment. "Do you need anything, T.J.?"

She didn't answer, but in a few moments, he saw the silver glisten of tears on her cheek.

She sniffed once, then wiped her hand across her cheek.

Jed handed her a clean towel. Then he put his hand on her back and gently stroked.

"Don't molly coddle me," she jerked.

"Why not?" he asked gently.

"Right now, I can't take it."

"Right now, you need it. You were very brave last night. You saved Mary's life- and your own. You don't have to be so brave now. Let us take care of you." He kept his hand on her back. He felt the quiver of her sigh.

She settled back into peaceful breathing.

Jed strained to keep from moving his hand, but when his leg cramped, he was forced to shift his position. His hand moved and she rolled back toward him.

Is she awake? He sat very still. She reached out her hand until she found his knee, then she sighed and was quiet again.

When her breathing became very regular, Jed placed his hand atop hers and laid his head back against the rocking chair. He slept too.

Dr. Andrews didn't disturb the pair, but in his sock feet, went upstairs to check on his other patient.

Shaker raised his head from the back of the chair and whispered, "Her night was restless, but she only needed one more dose of the medicine. Then she drifted off again. Sure glad you could come check on her during the night. Kind of made me nervous being here all alone and not knowin' what I needed to do the most."

Dr. Andrews laid his hand on Shaker's shoulder.

"Thank you, you're a good man. Have you ever thought about learning more about doctoring?"

Shaker started, "What do you mean?"

Dr. Andrews rubbed his morning stubble, "Been thinking about cutting back. I need a good man, wish you'd think about it."

Shaker stood, shook his head, too surprised to respond.

Dr. Andrews patted his shoulder, "You need a break, go on and get some air."

Shaker nodded, "I'll go make breakfast for everyone."

The long night had ended.

Recuperation came more slowly to Mary than to T.J. The younger woman sat up by late afternoon and by the end of the week, was making good progress. Her cough left during her indoor recuperation.

Mary spent hours with her leg propped. While she sat in her bed, Shaker was often in attendance.

Each day, they talked during these peaceful times after he brought her meals.

"Shaker, how old are you?" she asked.

"I'm thirty eight," he replied.

Mary was surprised. At first, she'd assumed he was a

very old man. His hair was salt and pepper and his stubbled face sported white whiskers.

"If you'd shave, I bet you'd look like a twenty year old," she remarked.

"Why would I want to do that?" Shaker asked.

"Perhaps you'd find a beautiful young lady who would think you were wonderful," she teased.

"Don't know why I'd want that. Been pretty happy the way things are. Jed's good to me."

"Didn't you ever want a family of your own?" she asked.

Shaker lowered his head.

Mary apologized, "I'm sorry. I shouldn't have asked that. It's really not any of my business."

"No, I'd like to tell you, Miss Mary. I had a wife once and we had a little boy." Shaker spoke, almost reverently.

Mary looked at his down turned head. She spoke gently, with honest concern in her voice, "If you don't mind me asking, what happened to them?"

"There was a cholera epidemic and they both went. It didn't matter what I did for them, I couldn't save them." His eyes reflected his stricken feelings for a moment, until he shook his head and looked away.

She raised her hand toward his shoulder. "I'm very sorry."

The pair were quiet..

Mary attempted to lighten the mood. "That must be why you're such a wonderful nurse."

"Just a horse doctor," he muttered.

She shook his shoulder, "You call me a horse, how dare you?" Mary teased.

"I didn't mean nothin' by that. I meant, I just have enough doctorin' to take care of a horse, or the most simple things."

"You're very good and I think you're a fine doctor." She bowed her head for a moment in thought. "Did you ever think of apprenticing to a real doctor and taking up the practice of medicine?"

Shaker seemed embarrassed. He rose and looked out the window.

"Doc Andrews mentioned somethin' 'bout that."

"You ought to consider it, two people thinking the same thing. Sometimes that's God's way of giving us a message, through other people." Mary hesitated, "If that's what you want."

"I better go get supper. I see the boys comin' in."

"Thanks, Shaker, you really might think about the doctoring."

He looked down, then raised his hand as he passed into the hallway.

Mary heard him descend the stairs. She had plenty of time to think. *An interesting man, much better educated than he lets on. His speech even changes when he's away from the men.*

The next time he brought her food, she noticed he was clean shaven and he did look much younger. *Put him in a suit, he'd be very distinguished. I'll feel him out and see what he really wants.*

Oh, Lord, don't let me meddle if this isn't your will. Strange both Dr. Andrews and I asked him about doctoring. Is that really your prompting for us to encourage him?

I've got too much time on my hands. Help me get well and out of this bed. Thank you, Lord. I will try to be patient.

Thank you that T.J. is doing so well; that she is able to take such good care of us both. On second thought, thank you for providing for both of us amongst all these men folk.

The next day, Mary heard a wagon rumble into the ranch yard. She rose slowly, hobbled to the window and looked out. Shaker drove the wagon, tied behind was a red and white cow, obviously a good milker.

Guess we haven't had much milk lately. The fellows haven't milked much, probably trying to feed that beast's calf.

Mary tottered back to her pillows. She didn't know about the deaths of *both* their milk cows.

When Mary could breath easily again, she read her Bible to Shaker while he sat in her room each afternoon after she ate her dinner.

Seven days after their disaster, when he left, she grew restless.

"T.J., the next time anyone comes upstairs, bring me some of that mending. I've done lots of Bible reading, but I'll go crazy if I can't do something to help out."

On Shaker's Saturday visit, he fidgeted.

"You have something on your mind?" she asked.

"Miss Mary, you know you talked to me about apprenticing? I talked to Dr. Andrews and he's agreeable to take me on to read medicine. He said he really does need someone and he thought I'd suit right well."

"That's wonderful!" Mary said.

"I won't be around as much, but Jed don't need a cook

when you ladies get well. T.J.'s almost back to doin' it all again and you won't be down much longer."

"I think I could peel potatoes and a few things now. Would you like to help me downstairs?" she asked.

"Miss Mary, are you sure?"

"Yes, very," she reached for his hand.

Shaker ducked his head. "I can carry you."

Mary thought, *He seems eager to carry me.*

"Just help me, I think I can walk if you do."

Shaker moved close and reached out. "Put your arm over my neck and we'll go down real slow. If you decide you don't want to, we can turn around and come back up."

Mary stumbled when she attempted weight on her injured ankle. "Maybe I had better let you carry me."

He lifted her into his arms and held her gently.

She inhaled deeply, *Cologne? Shaker smells good.* "What's your real name?"

"Adam Shumate."

That's a good solid name."

"Thankee, Ma'am."

He stumped down the stairs, walked to a chair with her and placed her gently in the seat. When she was settled, he pulled the stool over for her foot, adjusted a pillow and helped her get comfortable.

Mary breathed more heavily from her exertion.

"Give me a paring knife, some potatoes, and that pan with some water. Watch me go," then she laughed. "Oh," she put her hand to her right side.

"Does that still hurt?" Shaker asked.

"Only when I laugh." Mary looked into his concerned

face. "Thank you, you're a wonderful friend and you've taken good care of me."

He arranged the needed items and lingered uncomfortably, then hesitated and looked into her eyes.

He spoke breathlessly, "I better go now."

"Thank you- Adam."

Mary didn't miss the pleased look on his face when he turned to exit the kitchen. She smiled to herself. *Fine man, a very, kind, pleasant gentleman. Thank you, Lord, Thank you for- friends.*

Shaker started with Dr. Andrews the next week. He was better with the actual doctoring than he was with the books, but the pair made good progress. Dr. Andrews would be able to give him the knowledge and experience he couldn't gain directly from books.

Each Saturday, when he and the doctor weren't on call, Shaker came to the ranch. The whole ranch started driving in to church and stayed over in town until after they ate their basket lunch and enjoyed some afternoon visiting.

Shaker and Mary had become a pair, leaving Jed and T.J. the odd ones out. The younger pair were forced to be more tolerant of each other's company.

In very severe weather, no one traveled the roads, not wishing to experience a blizzard experience of the open plains.

Their relationships changed into an easier more comfortable arrangement for all.

Jed and Shaker talked one Saturday, "Did you see that Mexican bull toward town when you came out?"

"Yes, wonder where he came from, he isn't branded?" Shaker replied.

"He looks to be a four year old and tough as a buffalo

hide. I've said we needed some cross-breeding- expect we're getting it. I imagine his herd died off, but he survived the blizzards. Guess he got lonely and went to find some ladies," Jed guessed.

"Kind of like us, huh, Boss?" Shaker commented.

"Speak for yourself old man."

The two laughed with shared amusement.

Brand New Arrivals

Max hurried to Jed, "That Morgan mare has another horse colt. It's the ugliest little critter I ever saw."

"What's the matter with it?" Jed asked.

"He's high in the rear, never saw a colt built just like him. He's tough as nails though. He came out backwards but he never missed a lick. He's already nursed and his maw's proud of him," Max said. "He jumped her pile of hay as soon as he could walk. He's the fastest little dude I ever saw at this age and he has about as wild markings as you'll ever see."

Jed rubbed his day old stubble while he observed the Morgan and her new colt.

"Hard to tell much about them when they're so young. He'll change a lot in the next few months. His mother's a good one, so maybe he'll turn out better than he looks now. No telling what his paw was. He's got what Indians called *medicine hat* markings," Jed said. "He's definitely a mustang from his marking."

Max chuckled, "Look at them little guys go at each other. They sure got the mustang instinct. Already trying each other to see who's gonna be top herd boss."

Jed was preoccupied. "Leave them all in the corral next to the barn. We'll keep an eye on all the colts for the next few days, make sure they get a good start. Breeding will eventually tell on that Morgan- cross colt, unless there's a dud in there somewhere."

The next day, Jed hurried into the ranch house kitchen. "T.J. come with me, I've something to show you."

They went to the barn and turned to the first stall on the right.

T.J. saw Jed's buckskin mare. "I haven't seen you ride her lately, is she all right?"

"Look inside the stall and see what you think," Jed said.

T.J. stepped around Jed, he put his hand to the small of her back, as he swung the stall door open. Jed's buckskin mare rumbled deep in her throat, her head turned away from them.

"Oh- it's beautiful, and still wet," T.J. breathed.

"Just what I wanted, it's a filly," Jed said quietly.

"She is so beautiful, and- despite what I thought of Jones, she's marked just like his horse. Jed, is she?"

"Yes, she's out of Jones' horse. After Jones abused that horse at the races, I tried to buy him. Jones wouldn't give in, but I did persuade him to let us get a colt from his horse. Right after that, Jones sold the horse."

"I'm glad all the way around. Glad you got a colt," T.J. bubbled, "and glad that Jones won't be abusing that fine animal again."

"He didn't stay without a good horse long. He had the money and someone will always sell him another. He could have been through several by now," Jed said bitterly.

"At least this one's daddy is out of his control."

Jed watched T.J.'s face when she looked at the little filly nuzzling her mother.

T.J. turned to him, "Look at her trying to nurse. Your mare seems very proud of her. She is a beautiful sorrel."

Jed looked full into her face, his voice caught. He spoke before he thought, "You are beautiful"

T.J. startled. She turned into his arm, where it had remained on her back, "What did you say?"

Jed looked into her eyes. "I said, you are beautiful, T.J."

For once T.J. was shocked into silence.

Jed wrapped the fingers of his other hand around her upper arm. "T.J., I've thought you were the most beautiful thing to come into my life from the time I saw you trying to load that calf on our trail drive." He looked into her face, "Are you happy here?"

"I am happy," she sighed.

'But what?" Jed asked.

"You think you know me well, don't you?" she asked.

"Sometimes." He jerked his head, "T.J. don't change the subject- but what?"

"Oh, sometimes I feel lonely here." She looked down.

"I have that feeling too," he replied.

"Why?" she asked.

Jed looked resigned. "If I tell you, I run the risk of making you mad- or chasing you off."

"You have a right to your feelings too." She looked at him. "Tell me."

"Fine, here it is. You fit so perfectly into my life and you have such a good time doing it. I can't help but admire you. I'd like a family and everything that entails."

T.J. looked down. "A family. Yes, me too."

"Maybe that's why we feel lonely sometimes. Our lives aren't going anywhere. I know that I am taking advantage of you by using your money and now asking for more, but I can't go on with you at arm's length. Either we have to go forward, or I'll sell the cattle and get out. I can't stand still any longer." He looked full into her eyes, his own asking for an answer.

"This is too sudden, I don't know what to say," she said.

"Hardly sudden. We've worked together for over two years now," Jed said.

"Give me a little time," T.J. said.

"Sure." His hands fell away from her.

She shivered. *Cold, so cold where his hands were.*

Jed turned to the buckskin mare and her filly.

T.J. stared at his back, then turned toward the house and her room.

After his declaration, she spent hours in turmoil, either watching the new filly as she played; riding out alone; or staring into space.

When Jed rode out to work, she watched him go.

When T.J. moved about the place, Jed stared after her.

After three weeks, Mary could hold her tongue no longer.

"What's gotten into you? Anyone can see you two have a problem. You won't speak, but neither of you can carry on a simple conversation with anyone else. I never saw you so distracted. T.J., are you listening?"

"What?"

"What is the matter? You're not listening, or eating. Do you feel all right?"

Boss   -167-

T.J. grabbed Mary and hung on. "Jed said if we couldn't go forward, he'd sell the cows and leave."

"Do you want him to?" Mary asked.

"No-oh," T.J. sobbed.

"I imagine you could do something about it."

"What?" she asked.

Mary sighed. "Tell me exactly what he said."

"He said, he admired me. I fit into his life. That I had a good time on the ranch," T.J. paused.

"What else?" Mary prompted.

"He felt he was taking advantage of my money and now asking for more."

"What do you think he meant?" Mary asked.

"Well, he didn't want to be kept at arm's length anymore."

Mary laughed, "It's simple- he loves you and he wants to be with you. It's that simple, why make it so difficult?"

"I wasn't sure that was what he meant," T.J. sniffed.

"Why not?"

"I don't know," she wailed.

Mary patted her back. You are a miserable little thing aren't you? If you love him, all you have to do is give him a little encouragement. Quit being so stand-offish. A man wants a warm woman, not a boss like you've tried to be so often."

"How do I do that?" T.J. asked.

Mary put her hands on her hips, "Well, do you enjoy his company? If you do, invite him somewhere you two will be alone away from the rest of this bunch. Then be nice to him, but remember you are both Christian and you know how

Christians are supposed to act."

"Ye-yes," T.J. stuttered.

"Go think about it and see if you can come up with something that suits you," Mary advised.

"All right." T.J. wandered off toward the front porch.

An hour later, she returned with more resolve.

Mary looked at her determined face. "Did you come up with something?"

"Yes, I think I've got it now," T.J. said.

"Good, now can I quit worrying?" her aunt asked.

"Yes, but don't stop praying for us both." T.J. turned to leave.

"That's my girl. You pray too, and T.J.-   don't do anything too outlandish."

"Yes, Ma'am!" She looked at Mary and giggled.

"Uh-uh. You are going to pursue him?"

T.J. nodded her head in agreement, then whirled away.

Mary called after her, "Jed Snowden- here she comes, better get *ready or run.*"

T.J. spent the afternoon washing her hair. She carefully selected her most feminine dress. She applied dots of the toilet water her daddy gave her the last Christmas he lived.

She'd thought out her plans carefully. She knew Jed always put the buckskin mare and her filly to bed the last thing each evening. She entered the barn to find him bent over picking up a small hoof on the filly. She watched him as he spoke softly and gently raised each foot. The filly cooperated.

She can't resist his voice any more than I can, but she lets him touch her. Guess I could take a lesson from her.

T.J. stepped close to Jed. She spoke softly, "Hello,

she's really growing and you're doing a good job with her."

Jed stood up. T.J. was close. He brushed her with his elbow, then reached a hand out to steady her.

"Sorry, I bumped you."

Her hair brushed his cheek. He caught a whiff of summer lilacs. A picture of his childhood home flashed into his memory and then a longing for that kind of happiness. He looked into T.J.'s eyes in the lantern light. He lowered his hand.

She stared at him.

He waited patiently.

T.J. leaned closer.

Jed's lips descended to lightly contact hers.

T.J. stared into his eyes.

He looked into her face. *No surprise, no reaction.* She didn't resist.

Jed's arms went round her. He pulled her against him.

She leaned into his chest. Jed lowered his lips to hers again. "Do you know what you're doing?" he whispered against her cheek.

"Yes," she leaned into him. "Mary said I loved you, but I'm so stubborn, it took me a long while to know that she was right. Jed, I think I've loved you for a long while."

Jed brushed her lips with his own.

Ever her typical self, T.J. launched herself up on tiptoe and deepened their kiss.

Jed withdrew, breathless. He clutched her to his chest and groaned.

"You're torture. You never make it easy, but I wouldn't want you any other way. Will you marry me? And let's make it very soon."

"I thought you'd never ask," she grinned and reached for another kiss.

Later, they talked of their future partnership.

T.J. thought aloud, "Now it doesn't matter who is the boss, we *both* can run the ranch together."

Jed drew back to see if she was serious.

She giggled, "*You're* the boss."

He held her away from him, "*Remember that*, woman, the next time we have a disagreement."

She snuggled closer. "Oh, you *know* I will."

"Yeah, sure."

T.J. leaned in for another embrace.

Epilogue

T.J. framed their new rose bordered marriage certificate and hung it on the wall of the bedroom in *their* ranch house.

Shaker, now the respected Dr. Adam Shumate, and Mary Benton married soon after Jed and T.J.

The new doctor and his wife moved into town, but the couples made frequent trips back and forth to visit.

Every Sunday when the weather cooperated, was spent in each others' company.

When the babies arrived, each of the women assisted the other with the latest.

The town's newest doctor gained great experience in delivering babies, his own included.

The End

# # #

About the Author

Anita L. Allee lives near the small town of Versailles, in south central Missouri. She and Vincel are the parents of two grown daughters and five grandchildren.

Anita has a BS degree from the University of Missouri in Columbia. Her family and rural background enhance her knowledge of family relationships and animals.

The author may be contacted for further information on her books, experiential talks, or adult and school presentations at the following e-mail:

anviallee@earthlink.net

Previous Books:

Closed, Do Not Enter - historic fiction

Child of the Heart - historic fiction

Yankee Spy in New Orleans - historic fiction

High Country Adventure - contemporary fiction

76 Puppet Scripts - children's ministry